CAUGHT IN A HOT BOY'S *Flame*
The Baptist Brothers 2

A Novel By

TESHERA C.

© 2019 Royalty Publishing House

Published by Royalty Publishing House
www.royaltypublishinghouse.com

ALL RIGHTS RESERVED
Any unauthorized reprint or use of the material is prohibited. No part of this book may be reproduced or transmitted in any form or by any means, electronic or mechanical, including photocopying, recording, or by any information storage without express permission by the author or publisher. This is an original work of fiction. Names, characters, places and incidents are either products of the author's imagination or are used fictitiously and any resemblance to actual persons, living or dead, is entirely coincidental.
Contains explicit language & adult themes suitable for ages 16+ only.

Royalty Publishing House is now accepting manuscripts from aspiring or experienced urban romance authors!

WHAT MAY PLACE YOU ABOVE THE REST:

Heroes who are the ultimate book bae: strong-willed, maybe a little rough around the edges but willing to risk it all for the woman he loves.

Heroines who are the ultimate match: the girl next door type, not perfect - has her faults but is still a decent person. One who is willing to risk it all for the man she loves.

The rest is up to you! Just be creative, think out of the box, keep it sexy and intriguing!

If you'd like to join the Royal family, send us the first 15K words (60 pages) of your completed manuscript to submissions@royaltypublishinghouse.com

You a hot boy, a rock boy, a fun toy, tote a Glock boy.
 ~Missy Elliot

SYNOPSIS

I'm going to get each and every Baptist Brother if it's the last thing I do.

*W*hat was that saying? *More money more problems?* It seems like that is just it for the Baptist brothers, the more that they move up in life, trouble lurks in the shadows. Although they are ruthless in the streets and have built a successful empire, Sandy Muggs will stop at nothing to destroy them even if that means hurting the people closest to them and taking them each down one by one.

Flame is labeled as the street's *fire man*, not only because of his specialty, but because he was known for moving swiftly and never getting caught, that is until fate drops evidence in his arch enemies hands that could implicate him in the decade long mysterious house fire of his foster parents. Now, fighting for his freedom behind bars, Flame leans on his newfound love with Pia, unsure if she is strong enough to take this ride with him. With the lingering assumptions in his head, Flame finds himself gravitating towards his lawyer, Stephany Bianchi all in an attempt to get over Pia, but he soon learns that Pia has left an imprint on his mind that will be hard to erase. .

After having the love of his life, up and leave him for no apparent reason at all, Smoke finds himself in an obsessive state, desperate to find her. The constant merry-go-round that he feels they are on, has him hating Elle one day and longing for her return the next. Elle is just trying to maneuver through her hectic life by running and starting anew, after all, it is what she is good at. In her mind, all she has to do is step into herself and forget about the people in her past, but that proves to be an impossible mission as her heart still beats for a Baptist. Just as Elle finds herself adjusting to her new life, she meets a handsome stranger whose smile is not only breathtaking but deceiving.

Kiyan and Fancy are working to reconcile their differences so that they can raise their child together. While they work through their rocky relationship, the two are met with a person from Kiyan's past. Uncertain about this person's intentions, Fancy warns Kiyan, but just like a Baptist, he plays by his own rules, leading him to unveil the skeletons of is past that he may not be ready for.

In the final chapter of the Baptist saga, each brother finds himself giving into the idea of love, but this isn't a fairytale, so with the good comes the bad, and the Baptist brothers must figure out how to beat Muggs at her own game all while extinguishing the fires from their relationships

FLAME BAPTIST

*I*mages of me being picked up by Muggs flashed in my head. Simply walking down the street, I heard sirens in the distance, but I paid them shits no mind. I was good in every hood, so I didn't have anything to worry about. When the sound got closer, I turned around just in time to see five cars deep rolling up on me. I bit the inside of my jaw just thinking about how these niggas loved to fuck with me, but they would never have shit on me. That is, until I saw the biggest pig of them all.

"Well, well, well," I knew who she was before she could even show her face.

"Kindal, let's do this nice and easy," Muggs said, once she got out of her squad car, her gun aimed at me. Behind her were about ten other cops already for my black ass to make the wrong move. The red and blue lights illuminated in the half-lit sky making the passerby start to stop, pulling their phones out to record the show.

"Fuck do you want Muggs? I'm clean?" I stated, wishing that she would permanently remove, me and my bothers dick from her mouth. She hated the fact that her dad liked us over her butch looking ass so much that she tried to say that my brother raped her. The bitch had major issues.

Once she started to read me out my rights, my head dropped. My past was finally catching up with me, but how was the question. No one knew shit about that night so many years ago, but my brother's and me and I knew that they hadn't dropped the dime. I had set the Baptists house on fire with them in it and they deserved it.

"Kindal Baptist you ae being arrested on the charges of the murder of John and Mary Baptist. You have the right to remine silent," her voice trailed off as I half listened.

Cuffing me, I could feel her bad body ass smiling and It made me sick to my stomach, but I wouldn't give her the satisfaction.

"You want so Baptist dick in your rotten pussy so badly, that you pulled these dumb ass charges out of your ass, When I get out, I will gladly see what that mouf do," I smiled, right before she roughly pushed me into the back seat of her car.

"Kindal, you will never see that light of day once I'm finished with you and your Pansy ass brothers will be next," she said, before walking away.

That was exactly one month ago, and they had revoked my bail, leaving me here in jail. My lawyer who had gotten me out of numerous jams since I was seventeen was getting big bucks to get me out and so far, his ass wasn't doing his job; for the past few days, I hadn't even been able to get in contact with him. Shit was pissing me off and this nigga had twenty-four-hours to get in contact with me or his ass would be fired, and I would sick one of my brothers on his ass.

I felt a single bead a sweat fall from my head as I counted out my last few push-us. In this bitch I always had to stay ready and my stamina had to be up. Yeah, I was respected in the streets and in here, but there would always be the one person who tried some shit only to get knocked the fuck down. I finished up and grabbed the shirt off my thin mattress to wipe my face. My living quarters had changed vastly and now I had succumbed to living in a box like cell with only a mattress that felt like you were sleeping on a lawn chair and a toilet that did not flush.

Shit boggled me how I was even in this bitch. Word was that there was a recording of me saying some shit, but I wondered how. How in the hell would Muggs have access to anything that I had ever said, when the only people that I had talked to were my brothers? Shit ate me up, but I was glad that they were safe on the streets. If the shit came down to it, I would take the time, because I was the one who had did it. I would never compromise them or bring them into my shit knowing that they had their own lives.

⁓ My thoughts drifted to my girl Pia and for a minute I questioned her. She had been the only female that I had told about the house fire and just days after, I was being picked up by the police. She came to see me twice a week and every time I wanted to bring the shit up, I quickly erased it from my mind, knowing that that wasn't even her speed to be a snitch. She had spoken to me so many times about her four brothers and two of them were doing bids because of unroyal mutherfuckers, so I beat myself up for even blaming her in the first place. My mind would be at ease if my bitch ass lawyer got on his shit. If there was a recording, the person who had the audacity to record it should be made to eat it.

I laid back with my hands tucked under my head. Like the typical nigga, I wondered it Pia would play her part. I knew we hadn't been kicking it for too long, but I wondered if she would ride this shit out with a nigga. I didn't know what my fate would be fucking with Muggs so them twenty-one questions that fifty cents had were now floating through my mind. I couldn't hold Pia back from anything because she still had to live her life, but I didn't want her to. Shit may sound selfish, but it was scary for me to think about her moving on without me. She was the first woman that I had ever loved, and I wanted her with me even if it was only through phone calls and visits. I needed her.

PIA KENNEDY

I fumbled inside of my purse trying to dig for my phone, but it seemed like I was pulling out everything but it from lipstick to tampons. My bag then dropped, exposing all the remnants inside and when I finally got to my phone, I had missed the call.

"Dammit!" I shouted, stomping my feet like a child. This was the second call from Flame that I had missed, and I knew that the phones would be cutting off soon. Earlier, I had stepped away and missed his call and now, something so simple as having a messy purse had done it. I piled the things back into my bag and made it inside of my home a little disappointed.

Almost tripping over something that lay casually on the floor, I dropped my things and slammed down onto the couch. Today had been the longest day from hell and I knew that I would have to hear Flame's mouth in the morning for missing his calls. Lately things had been so hectic with him going to jail, and me just trying to handle it all; everything was just happening so fast. People just didn't understand that dealing with a person in jail was a job in itself. I was expected to visit him weekly, put money on the phone for call, speak with lawyers, send packages, and overall help to keep his spirits up with everything that he was going through.

Aside from tending to an inmate, I still was living out in the real world and had to work. All of Flame's accounts were frozen and though he had stashed money, that he told me to dip into more than once, I knew that that was not something that I was willing to do. I didn't want him to think that I was just with him for his money or that I was incapable of taking care of myself, so HIS money went solely to him.

I got up from the couch after about thirty minutes of just starring. My house wasn't going to clean itself and I had been living in filth for the past few weeks. I kicked off my stilettos and turned on my music to hear Beyoncé's *Brown Skin Girl*. Being a brownie myself, I really connected with the song and it could get me out of the funkiest of moods. I swayed to the beat as I picked up the work clothing and numerous shoes from the floor. Lately the living room had been my room simply because I had been so drained and couldn't make it to my bedroom.

Loading the dishes into the dish washer and staring to vacuum the floor, I started to feel a little better that that my living space wasn't so cluttered. They said that your home reflected who you were and honey, my house had definitely been a place of confusion and clutter for me lately. Once, I was satisfied with my progress, I headed to tackle my bedroom which wasn't so bad besides the clothing that needed to be thrown in the hamper. Removing the clothing that I currently had on, I started my shower and knew after that intense cleaning session and a warm shower, I would be knocked out like a baby.

Just as I stepped into the shower, I heard my phone ring and from the time on my apple watch, I knew that it wouldn't be Flame calling so late. I started to just let it ring, but my curiosity got the best of me. I wrapped a towel around my waste and jogged to my bedroom. The phone was still ringing and I scrunched my face up when I saw that the number was blocked. I ended the call and my phone automatically started to ring again and this time I decided to answer.

"Hello!" I answered full of attitude. I couldn't hear anything on the other end but breathing.

"Hellllooooooo!" I said, once more just before I was about to hang up.

"He hello," the voice said lowly, but no matter how low it was I knew exactly who it was.

"ELLE! Elle ifs that you?" I asked, surprised. No one had heard from her in weeks. It was like she had dropped off the face of the earth.

"Yeah, it's me."

"Elle, where in the hell have you been? You know how worried Smoke has been.. how worried I have been!"

"I know I Know, but I had to get away." Elle was still low. She already had a tiny voice, but she sounded different and it worried me.

"Elle tell me where you are. I will come and get you right now," I assured her.

"Pia, I can't. Not right now. I got myself into some shit."

"What kind of shit that would make you up and leave. I'm sure whatever it is, Smoke can help you with it."

"Pia just listen. I'm not coming back, but I wanted to reach out to you, because I consider you a friend. I am okay."

"Elle, whatever it is. I am here for you. I know we haven't known each other long, but I got you. You need money or anything?"

When she didn't answer I knew it was her pride that wouldn't let her.

"Look, I'm going to western Union your money tomorrow. I don't even need to know where you are, all you have to do it go to the nearest one okay and be safe Elle."

With that she let out a thank you and I could tell that she was crying right before she hung up.

I held the phone to my chest for a minute wondering what could be so bad that she felt the need to run. Day in and Day out, Smoke had been worried about her and I didn't have anything to tell him. The smile that was constantly plastered on his face had disappeared and he had become someone hardened. A blind man could tell that he loved Elle and was disappointed in her for just up and leaving, but now I knew that she had a reason and even though I didn't know the reason, he secret was safe with me.

SMOKE BAPTIST

I sat on the floor in the lotus position as my girls Salt and Puff just stared on with their tongues hanging out of their mouths. Finally closing my eyes, I focused on my breathing and tried to block out all the ramped thoughts that were going through my head. If I wasn't thinking about Flame, then Elle was running through my mind all day. At first, I wondered where she was, I even tried looking for her, but now, I didn't give a fuck about what where she was. Just to up and leave was some weird shit. Then a part of me wondered if she was kidnapped or something, but I quickly erased that knowing that no one would be dumb enough to touch something that belonged to a Baptist.

When I went to her house and seen that half of her closet was empty, I knew that this was something that she had planned, but the question that would always linger within me, was why? No matter how hard I acted of how badly I wanted to kill her ass, I wondered why she had just up and left. She and I were getting serious and I wondered if that scared her or something. Baby girl didn't have to handle it like this though.

I exhaled through my mouth and inhaled again through my nose. The Lox played in the background because even though I was into meditating, I was still a gangster'. I then laid back bringing my knees up to my chest and holding them, again Elle would not leave mt mind. Out of all the other things that I had to be worried about, she would never leave my mind.

I finished up my mediation, just in time to see the sun rising. I filled my girl's bowls so that they could stop following me everywhere and then I went to shower. With Flame being locked up, I was working overtime at the barbershop just to keep me from exploding inside. They had revoked his bond and now it was just a waiting game. I couldn't wait until the nigga got out because he called me all day every day and he was constantly worrying me about what Pia was doing. That girl handled her business and that was none of my business.

I walked into Smokin' Kuts which was at its normal capacity, with people waiting from the front to the back. The summer was almost over so the weather was still warm, and it wasn't the time yet that niggas could rock their untamed beards and haircuts. Though the shop was packed, there was a sadness the sept into the air. Pops would no longer be able to sit in his designated chair and talk shit because he was no longer with us. The doctors said that it was a heart attack and the crazy thing about it was, by the time we had found out that he had passed, his bitch ass daughter had already had a service and got him cremated. That shit hurt me to my core that she was so damn evil.

Muggs never liked me or my brothers so I don't even know why I expected her to ,do anything different than be a jealous ass person with hatred in her heart. Muggs was a few marbles short, and for some reason back in the day, she thought that I liked her. The crazy lady had the audacity to say that I raped her, but that shit didn't get far after Pops found where she had written an entire plan to get me and my brothers out of the picture, all because I had rejected her. Every time I would come over Pops house just to chop it up with him, there she would be hawking me down. I ignored her hot ass until, one day I came there, and pops left us alone. I had to be about nine-teen, twenty and she was like seventeen.

I walked to the kitchen to get something to drink and when I walked back to the living room, baby girl had come down in a towel dripping wet. Like the typical nigga, I indulged when she dropped the towel to the ground, admiring her developing body. She didn't have much up top and was average looking in the face, but that ass was something to talk about, damn near sitting on her back. She walked up to me with this look in her eye and as bad as my dick was jumping, I knew that I couldn't do this to Pops. This slow ass girl was the apple of his eye and yeah, I wanted my dick sucked, but I had a feeling that this would be more than just a sexual encounter to Sandy.

"Yo', I'm not even about to take it there with you Shorty," I said, backing up and taking a sip from the water bottle that I was holding.

"I want your dick in every one of my holes," she said, seductively all the while walking up closer to me.

"Whoaaa girl! Calm yo' ass down. I'm not fucking you. I have too much respect for your pops to drag you like that. You need to get back in the shower and this time make it a cold one," I walked around her headed to the front door. I would just have to catch pops another time.

"Wait!" she rushed up to me. "What? I'm not good enough for you or something?"

I bit the inside of my jaw to keep from laughing in her face. "I'm out of here. Go put some damn clothes on Sandy."

"Well fuck you too. I don't even know what I was thinking anyway. Your dick probably tastes like struggle and poverty anyway. Bye bone thugs and harmony."

"Bye single black female," I waved her deluded ass off before chuckling to myself, not knowing that she would later try to say that I raped her.

I got my workspace ready and prepared myself for the dozens of heads that I would be cutting today and the assignment that I was preparing for and these hands had to be in tip top shape. I peeped Pia walking in and in my usual fashion I gave her a welcoming head nod, but unlike any other day, she avoided eye contact with me and whizzed by, no hello, no nothing. That was a little weird, because Pia was one of that mouthy kind of woman who never had nothing to say. I picked up on the way she was moving, and I knew that she had been purposely avoiding me, but why, was the question.

ELLE LONDON

I rounded the corner, pulling my cap tightly over my eyes. The sun was beaming down on me and with each step I took I exhaled a huge breath, tired after only taking a few steps. I turned around swiftly trying to be mindful of my surroundings. It had become a habit of mine, looking behind my back everywhere that I went, afraid that someone could snatch me up at any moment. I had been holed up at my parents for the past few weeks thinking about my next move. I could not stay long because people would suspect that it would be the first place that I would go so now I had to think about where I would go next.

I entered the western union inconspicuously and typed in my name and the code word that I had got rom Pia. I knew that I could trust her, but I was also a little scared that she would slip up and say something, so that is why I didn't tell her where I was. When she found out that I was the reason her man was in jail anyway, she would for sure hate me and tell the other brothers. Me being so careless, I had fucked up and trusted Muggs, only for her to do what I knew she would do.

When I first saw on every major news outlet that Flame had been arrested, I knew that I would not be returning to Virginia. I didn't know exactly what the Baptists were capable of, and I damn sure wasn't going to stick around to find out. The entire situation was not even my fault, but who would want to hear that knowing that I was being sneaky in the first place and was working with Muggs. If I would have never listened to Muggs, there wouldn't even be a recording and Flame would be home with his family, but no, I had to be the one who did the dumb shit.

I Grabbed the three hundred dollars that Pia sent me and I closed my eyes and said a silent prayer, thanking her. She didn't know how much I needed it so that I could get on the road to leave. I had a cousin in Ohio, so that was an option for me, and I just had to get there and then I would attempt to start my life over.

After walking one hundred miles per hour, I was finally home at the house that held so many memories for me. When I first came back, I thought that my parents would be mad at me for staying away for so long, but they welcomed me with open arms. I couldn't believe that I had stayed away for so long all because of Que, but my family didn't make me feel bad for falling in love. Even my room was still the same. They hadn't touched a thing, my canopy bed was still there, all made up and pretty. My collage of pictures was still taking up and entire wall and my vanity set was like it was sitting waiting for me. It felt so nostalgic to be back in the room that I had experienced so much. Back in the day I had even snuck one little boy up in my room and he called himself popping my cherry, but it never happened.

Then one day, my neighbor's cousin had visited, and he couldn't keep his eyes off me. He only stayed over the summer, and from then on, we were connected and I moved with him after I graduated highschool and now here I am back again. Just as I sat down on my bed ready to lay it flat, I heard my father calling me. I was tired as heck all from that little walk and here my daddy came being worrisome. I cascaded the winding stair well in our middle-class home to see that my dad was in the living room reading the paper. When he saw me, he put it away and patted the seat next to him. For a moment he only looked at me and I wondered what he was thinking about. There still was so much that hadn't been said between us like why I had stayed away for so long and why I was back.

"Baby girl," he started. His tone warm and hearty, but concerned, nonetheless. "You know me and your mother have loved having you back home and you know that you will always have a home here with us, but we are worried about you. You seemed troubled. Tell your old man what is going on," he softly caressed my hand.

I looked down and started to play with my hands, fearful of telling him my truth. To be honest I just didn't want to trouble them and in order for me to not do that I knew that I had to leave. I knew that by leaving, it would only upset my parents again, but my biggest fear was bringing them any harm. I would die if anything happened to them or if I were to ever put them in harm's way.

"Daddy, it's a lot. I have just been through some things, but I never wanted to let you and mama know because I thought that you would be ashamed. Y'all didn't rise me to be like this," I quickly wiped away the tears that began to fall from my eyes.

"Elle, do you know how proud I have always been to be your father. You know that you were always my number one girl. Since you were knee high, you never gave me and your mother any problems. We kept waiting for the other shoe to drop, but it never did. You are and always have been perfect to me. Whatever you've been through will only make you stronger and whenever you are ready to talk I will be here, but I am glad that you are home," he said, assumingly.

Maybe that was my problem. I had been so busy trying to live up to everyone's materialist standards, that I had somehow sabotaged myself. My dad had just described me as perfect and that made me cringe a little. I was far from perfect and he ever learned about some-things that had done in my past, his perception of me would definitely change.

He pulled me in for an embrace and I melted in his arms. The water works wouldn't stop and I knew that now I couldn't stay no matter how badly I wanted to. I wouldn't let them get attached to me only for me to have to leave.. again. That night I fell asleep in my father's arms with a heavy heart and dancing mind. I cried out for

Smoke who I knew that I had let down. Every day I thought about him and whether I should have just been up front with him and told him the truth. I wondered how he was holding up and if he was still connected to my soul like I was his.

Many times, I could feel him, his aura still lingering around me. Even times, I would randomly smell him, his strong yet sweet scent overwhelmed me to the point that it brought tears to my eyes. Smoke was the only man who had ever loved me the way that a man was really supposed to, and we were so good, but ended so quickly. Knowing that I would never see him again cut me like a knife that wouldn't stop bleeding.

KIYAN BAPTIST

I weaved in an out of traffic hoping that I made it on time. My shift at the hospital had ran a little long pushing me back an entire hour. I had one more year and then I would start my three-year fellowship. I loosened my tie and looked down at my GPS which said that I had about fifteen minutes until I reached my destination. I would cut down that time to at least seven minutes. Beating the GPS for me was like and extreme sport and I won every time.

Rounding the corner of a nice community with single and multi-homes, I pulled up to a two-story red brick one. In the driveway, I spotted the car that I was looking for and immediately hopped out. I walked into the home without even announcing my presence and I could hear Fancy's voice in the distance. I climbed the staircase and found her standing in the hallway with two older women. When Fancy saw me, she smiled politely at the two women and then excused herself by walking down the stairs with me following behind her.

"Kiyan, what are you doing here?" she asked, lowly hoping that her clients would not hear.

"Well, since you can't answer your phone, I decided to come and find you."

"What do you want? You know when the next doctor's appointment is, so I'm confused."

I looked down at Fancy's growing belly and it made me smile a little. She was almost five months pregnant and soon we would be finding out the sex of the baby, but Fancy was leaning towards not learning the sex until she had the baby. Fancy and I were still separated and after finding out that I was fucking Shay she had once again iced me out. No gift or sorry was getting her to come back home this time, but I wouldn't take any of that bullshit for an answer. Whether she liked it or not, we were still married and as far as I was concerned, we were going to stay that way.

"Uhhh hello, earth to dumb ass!" she snapped. These days she was very spicy. I remember the days when she would t utter a curse word.

"Faye, you are making this really difficult for me and I know that you are still bitter about the things that happened in our past but I'm here to tell you that I am not giving up. Our kid will have its mother and father TOGETHER," I made a point to highlight the *together* part.

"Kiyan, coming and stalking me at my job isn't going to make me hate you any less."

"Hate is a strong word Faye. Watch that shit!"

"No, you watch it and don't ever come to my to where I work again unless you are buying a house."

"As if I can't, I will buy a block of these mutherfuckers," I shouted ,not caring If her clients heard. Fancy called herself trying to hide her smile as she raised her hand to cover my mouth. This was the first time that she had gave me any other type of emotion besides just being mean as hell.

Just then, the two women emerged down the stairs and the lighter one with the silver hair stopped for a moment.

"Do I know you from somewhere young man?" she asked, while holding her finger at her chin as if she was trying to recall something.

"No, I don't believe so," I commented politely.

"Candis, come one. That young whipper snapper does not want you," her friend joked.

"I don't either, so she can have him." Fancy joined in on the laughter, but that shit was not funny to me.

I went to leave so that she could finish showing the women the rest of the house, but not before reminding her ass of why I had rushed there in the first place. "Answer your phone Faye or these pop-up's will become more frequent."

"Find you some business Kiyan and just for the record, I'm not bitter, I'm angry as hell."

She corrected me and just like that all of the laughter that had just happened to minutes earlier was gone. The scowl that was permanently connected to her face these days returned and she turned her back on me. All I could do was shake my head, but there was still some hope left for us. Fancy hadn't mentioned the big D word yet, so I figured that's she wasn't ready to throw the towel in just yet. I just had to work a little bit harder to get my girl back and whatever I had to do; I would do it.

FLAME BAPTIST

I waited in the room with nothing but a metal table, concrete walls and cement floors. The room was cold as shit, so I guess they was trying to freeze a nigga or something when I didn't even know why I was here. I rested my head on the equally as cold table when the door suddenly swung open. In walked a short mixed looking chick. She looked at me intently before shutting the door behind her and sitting her brief case down on the table. She looked at me again before taking a seat and smoothing out her tailored pants.

"Fuck are you?" I finally spoke up tired of her staring in my damn face without saying anything.

"Nice to meet you too Kindal. I am Stephany Bianchi and I will be handling your case from now on. My father passed away two days ago," she said, with no emotion whatsoever in her face for someone who had just lost their dad.

Damn so that why that nigga ain't been answering his phone. My thoughts went back to how many times I had tried to reach my lawyer in the past couple of days and come to find out the nigga had croaked. I would definitely miss him. He had handled every one of my cases helping me to get out each and every time.

"I'm sorry to hear about your pops and all, but I don't need you to take my case."

She held her hand up to silence me. "Look, my father knew that he was sick, so he educated me on all of his cases. I know about you and your brothers inside and out I am more than capable of handling this case and right now you need me," she said, with a sharp tone.

I looked at her and rubbed by chin before speaking hoping that she heard me loud and clear. "I don't need you for shit. You come walking in here like you fucking running shit so as much as your pops told you about me, he obviously didn't tell you that I'm the one that gives zero fucks. Now walk yo' cocky ass out of here the same way you just came in. fuck wrong with you!"

Stephany now looked like she was getting somewhat flustered which let me know that she needed my case more badly than I needed her to take it. She had the audacity to say that I needed her like my brothers and me weren't sitting on millions and could hire the nigga who got OJ off.

"Mr. Baptist, I think that we got off to a wrong start here," she started.

"No, you got off to a wrong start and I'm not about to let you fuck up my case all because you got something that you need to prove. Now, tell me why you really want to defend me and if you come with that bullshit you tried earlier; you may as well make your exit," I pointed to the door.

Stephany removed her blazer and let out a sigh. "You are right, I need you, but hear me out. Like I know about your family, I'm sure you have heard of mine, hence the reason you chose my father out of all people to represent you. My father had been going through things with his heart since he was child and had over one hundred surgeries. Even with me knowing his health condition, I was a fuck up. I was a major fuck up, rebelling at a young age, doing dumb shit that he had to pay to get me out of from trying drugs, being promiscuous and other questionable things. So, my dad got really sick about a year ago and instead of me getting my shit together, I was still fucking up."

She started to tear up but hurriedly wiped away her falling tears.

"So, I didn't come here to get into all of this with you, but I just really need this. I wasn't the daughter that I needed to be for my father when he was here, but I want to show him that I can be better and do better," she finished.

I smirked a little at her story. It's not that I didn't feel her, but I wasn't the daddy that she was looking for.

"So, let me get this straight. I'm facing fed numbers for murder and you expect me to let you hop on my case so that you can rid yourself of the guilt of you being the person who put your old man in his early grave?" I stroked my chin and her mouth dropped.

"That will never happen Pooh. You want to right your wrongs; you have to do that on someone else's case. I'm not wasting my time on my money on a recovering addict who calls herself a Lawyer in a desperate attempt to get close to a Baptist. It's going to be a hard no for me sweetheart," I dismissed those tears that threatened to fall down her eyes and stood up to let the guards know to get me the hell away from this bitch.

If her father couldn't represent me, I would just have to find someone else of his stature and reputation, if not better. I had to make a mental note to get one of the other Baptist's to send his family some flowers or some shit. I glanced back at shorty right before I exited and she just sat there with her head down defeated, but that was not my problem. These women needed saving and I was not going to be the one to do it.

PIA KENNEDY

"Hello," I spoke into the phone somewhat groggy from being woken up out of my sleep. I looked at the clock and it was 9:04 pm and I couldn't believe that I had been knocked out since around four pm after I finished up with my last client.

"Yo! Fuck type of time you on!" I instantly noticed Flame's voice from the way he barked and I had to sit up and look at the phone because I was genuinely confused.

"Hello!" I said, again hoping that he would correct his tone.

"You heard me! Why do I have to call you thirty times for you to answer like I have that type of liberty or something."

Shit!

Now I knew why the nigga was snapping. I had managed to fall asleep missing his phone calls two consecutive days in a row. I wasn't doing the it on purpose, but mama had been tired.

"Helloo," I was so damn exhausted that I repeated myself for the third time.

"Say hello one more fucking time!" he yelled, into the phone. Little did he know that his hollering and brash tone was not even fazing me.

"I'm great Flame, how are you?" I sarcastically asked.

"This is not the time to be smart Pia. What's going on with you?

You avoiding me or something?" The hardest men on the streets were always in their feelings once they got behind that G-wall.

"Flame, we have just been missing each other. I'm not avoiding you, but we're talking now so there is no use in wasting it on arguing for the entire phone call," I got up from the bed and went to splash some cold water on my face so that I could wake up a little.

"You have to tighten up Pooh. I just be missing you. It feels like shit doesn't even go right for me when I don't talk to you. How you been though?" he asked, calming down some.

"Just trying to maintain. I miss you too though bighead. Did you hear anything back from your lawyer?"

"Man, you won't believe this shit. The nigga is dead and his daughter came up here today talking about she wants to represent me today."

"And what is wrong with that?" I sensed that he was skeptical.

" I'm just not with it. That's all."

"So, you want me to start looking for new lawyers?" That would just be another thing added to my plate.

"Nah, I talked to Kiyan today and he is already on it."

I let out a silent sigh of relief and then finally got up from the toilet before my feet started to fall asleep.

"So, what is going on with you for real. You sound different." Flame must've picked up on my mood.

To be honest, I couldn't pinpoint what was really wrong, but I just didn't think that months into her getting with Flame, that he would have to go to jail changing the dynamic of our relationship. I hadn't been in a relationship in a while, but when I was, I loved hard. Not being able to emotionally feel Flame or physically touch him was getting to me a little and I doubted if I could be the woman that he needed me to be while he was away.

"Nothing is going on with me," I lied. "I am great, just a little tired," I called myself perking up a bit. "But guess what though?"

"What?"

"I'm about to start taking all of your clients."

"Says who?" he let out a chuckle.

"Says me. I'm learning how to cut now and pretty soon I'ma be a beast with the clippers pooh!"

"Girl you wish," he laughed "You better stick to do doing lashes." Flame knew that he was the best barber around town, and he wore that title proudly.

I laughed so hard. "Screw you! You know damn well I don't do lashes. That's like comparing me to a bottle girl or something."

"Girl, I know what you do. You jack people eyebrows up."

"I'ma jack you up! Keep playing with me."

"Nah, but for real though, I'm glad you decided to answer the phone for me today. I know you busy and all, but it's nice to know you put some time aside for your man."

For some reason, Flame was covering up his snide remarks with joking when he really was serious about the little jokes that he was making. "Umm, I know you mean that as a joke and all, but it's not funny. I don't purposely ignore you. Actually, you and your needs consume most of my day."

"Damn, well tell me how you really feel."

"I just did," I said shortly. Just that quick he had managed to say something stupid to throw my entire mood off.

"Aite man, I'm gone."

"Wait, wait, I'm sorry. I'm doing too much right now. Gimme kiss," I said, sweetly into the phone. I didn't want to end our call on a bad note, so I sucked my feelings up.

"What?" he asked, like he didn't head me the first time.

"Put you lips together and give me a kiss!"

"Girl, gone head. Savages don't do that type of stuff."

"Well, this savage better do it if he wants a visit this week."

Flame then blew a raspberry before I finally head the sound of him pursing his lips together and making the kissing sound. I smiled deeply knowing that he only did it because I asked no matter how much he didn't want to. We ended the call five minutes later and like a light I was out soon after.

SMOKE BAPTIST

"Man, you just get yo' ass back here soon," I said, into the phone. Iggy had been coupled up on some island with Beau ever since she had been discharged from the hospital and like the big brother that he was, he was constantly calling me checking on everything and making sure that things were good with the brothers and the shop. He had even hired a doctor and a nurse to travel with them since Beau was still going through chemo. He protested about going at first because of Flame's situation, but in the end, I talked him into going letting him know that I could handle the home front. Him and Beau needed this time and with him gone he could fly under the radar from Muggs.

"Boy, I don't even want to leave. Might got to buy another house over here or something," Iggy replied, referring to the Caymans Island where him and Beau were.

"Yeah, you and Beau living y'all best lives while I'm holding shit down at the shop. It's all good though," I chucked. "But bruh hit me later. 'Bout to handle some shit really quickly."

"Aite, Aye! Did you hear from the girl yet?" I knew exactly who Iggy was asking about.

"Nah, but I'm not even stunning that. It is what it is!"

"Word!"

"Bye Shameeer!" I heard Beau in the background rushing us of the phone.

I smiled and ended the call just in time when I was pulling up to a modest two-story home with a Station wagon parked in the driveway along with a Dark Blue updated minivan. I checked the time to see that I had been driving for six hours non-stop all in an attempt to get some answers. I walked up to the home and for the first time ever in my life I was nervous. I rang the doorbell before talking myself out of it and I heard a woman sing .

"Cooommmiiinnng!" her high-pitched voice rang out sounding like the actress Loretta Divine.

The door swung open, without so much as a who is it and it must've been because she lived in this cookie cutter ass neighborhood.

"Can I help you?" she asked, wiping her hands across the apron that was around her waist.

"Hi, my name is Shameer and I was looking for—" my words got a little lost when my eyes zoned in the house and on the coffee, table was a charm bracelet with multiple elephants on it. Different elephant charms of different colors were on the bracelet and then I knew that Elle was here. Elle loved elephants claiming that they were the gentlest animals and how she worked at the zoo one summer and had loved the elephants ever since. She wore that damn bracelet everywhere.

"Excuse me son are you okay?" the woman asked once she noticed that I was staring somewhat gazed.

I snapped out of it quickly. "Um I'm sorry. Is Elle available?"

The women's shoulders slumped, and she suddenly backed away from me. "If you are of any relation to that Muggs person, you will not find her here. Just leave my baby alone!" she shouted trying to shut the door.

"Hold on ma'am, I can assure you, I'm not." My mind was now racing trying to figure out why this woman who I presumed to be Elle's mom would think that I had anything to do with Muggs and how in the hell did Elle even know her.

"What's going on out here?"

An older man with salt and pepper hair said as he emerged from the back of the house.

I held up my hand in surrender knowing how it looked that this random man was just knocking on the door looking for their loved one.

"Look, I promise I'm not here to start anything or hurt Elle. I was just worried about her because I haven't seen her and just wanted to make sure that she is good."

"And who are you? The way your eyes light up when you say my daughter's name makes me think that y'all were more than friends," the man commented.

I wiped my hand over my face and forced a smile. "We were very good friends, but I see that she is not here so I'ma bounce."

I turned to walk away wondering why I had even set myself up for this dummy mission. Elle was pissing me the fuck off quite frankly.

"Wait!" I heard the woman call out against the man's judgment.

"Our daughter was here up until last night and before then we hadn't seen her in over five years."

I turned around to see the pained look on her faced and I could tell that she was genuinely concerned about her daughter like I was. To know that I was so close to seeing her got to me as well. She had left only a few hours before I arrived and now, I had no clue as to where she could be going.

"We don't know where she ran to this time. Just when we were getting to know her again, she up and left, but she kept saying she didn't want to hurt us and I heard her on the talking in her sleep about someone names Muggs and something about a house fire, but I don't know what she was talking about."

Now my wheels were really turning. Why would Elle be talking about a house fire in connection with Muggs. Now I knew that I had to get to Elle, because if she was involved in anything with Muggs, she definitely was playing for the other side and well,. .that wouldn't end too well for her.

"Would you like to come in?" the woman asked. She seemed like she was looking for answers just like I was, but I didn't have any to give her.

Against my better judgement, I found myself walking into the home and immediately I knew that Elle was loved. The numerous pictures of her that were plastered on the wall let me know. Pictures from her sand box age to when she went off to the prom let me see how she had developed so beautifully.

"You can have a seat son," her father said.

"You said your name was Shameer right. Well I am April, and this is Edward. Would you like anything to drink?"

"No thank you," I said, not really wanting to overstay his welcome.

"Well, we don't really know what to tell you son, but our daughter was just here for a few weeks until she left last night without me or my wife knowing. I don't know what is going on with her, but she is troubled. She is running from something and I can bet my last dollar that it has something to do with that no-good Que boy. Ever since she got with him years ago, he kept her from us and put he through so much. He's in jail now, but I feel like he has something up his sleeve."

I took in all that her parents had to say and just as I was about to make an excuse to get up out of there, the front door opened and in walked a girl who had an uncanny resemblance to Elle. She was just an inch taller and a shade lighter.

"Maaaammmaaa!" she yelled out before fully making it to the living room.

"Eboni, do you have to be so loud all of the time?" April asked.

Eboni ignored her mother and looked down at me. A smile instantly appeared on her face and I could see the lust in her eyes.

"And who is this?" she asked.

"Ohhh, this is your sister's friend Shameer," Edward answered.

"Ohhh, so you know run away barbie. Where did she run off to this time?" Ebonie asked with a twinge of disappointment in her voice.

"That's what I'm trying to figure out," I said. "But I'm about to get on the road back home to VA. I was a pleasure meeting you all and if I hear from Elle, y'all will be the first to know."

I shook Edwards hand and gave April a hug before making my exit. As I was getting into my car the front door opened and it was Eboni. She jogged up to the car and I rolled down the window. I hoped that I wouldn't have to bust this little girl's fucking bumble if she was on some slick shit.

"Sooo, I don't know if you know this or not, but my sister is very delicate unlike me and that was the whole reason that Que controlled her for so long. Whoever this Muggs person is, he or she definitely has something on my sister that she feels the need to run, and though Elle sometimes does dumb shit, she has good intentions and a good heart," she finished.

"So, why you are telling me all of this?" I asked, blatantly.

"Because I want you to know that if you find out somethings that you may not expect from her, her intention is to never hurt anyone. If anything, she would hurt herself first." With that Eboni smiled and then walked back towards the house leaving me even more confused that I had been before I arrived. If I couldn't find Elle, then I would have to talk to another name that seemed to just keep popping up in my life. Sandy Muggs.

ELLE LONDON

I settled into my seat and braced myself for the long bus ride ahead of me. I shifted back and forth in my seat trying to get comfortable, but the more I shuffled the more uncomfortable I became. I let out a long sight before finally just sitting straight up and laying my blanket across my lap. I felt for my left wrist and not feeling what I was looking for I instantly jumped up. Trailing my entire arm, I felt for my bracelet and it wasn't there.

I suddenly hoped out of my seat and went to look in my bag which was in the overhead bin and after minutes of rummaging, I realized that it was not there. I instantly started to panic, and I felt like the air in my lungs was slowly seeping away from me. I ran to the entrance of the bus and jumped down not even bothering to use the steps. My parents had given me that bracelet on my fifteenth birthday and it had got me through some of the toughest times.

"Yo' you good?" I felt a strong grip around me.

"Yes, I'm fine," I said, breaking from his hold and when I finally looked up, I was met with the eyes of a handsome stranger. My eyes went straight to his long lashes that most women would kill for and the pearly whites that he displayed paired with his midnight colored skin.

"You dropped this," he said, handing me my bag.

"Thank you," I replied, slowly still a little mesmerized at the person standing before me who I had practically knocked to the ground from running off the bus.

"You sure you okay?" he asked.

"Yes. I'm sure. Thank you again!" I said, turning to walk away.

When I turned around, he was gone, and I took the time to take in the night air. My thoughts then drifted to my parents and how worried they probably were. I had snuck off into the night knowing that my time had come to an end with them. If Muggs was looking for me to testify or just to fuck with me she would know where to come and just in case Smoke wanted to blow my head off for what I had did to his brother, I knew that I had to go. I would call my parents as soon as I got settled in Ohio with my cousin.

About ten minutes later, the driver let everyone who hadn't boarded the bus that we would be leaving in ten minutes, so I took that as my cue to get on the bus. I walked slowly to the back; my head low afraid to look the people who had just saw me storm off the bus in their eyes. When I finally reached my seat, I was surprised to see the man who I had just briefly met. He was sitting with his eyes closed with air buds in his ears. I didn't want to disturb him but, I need to get my seat and his muscular frame was preventing me from doing so.

I gently tapped his knee, and those long lashed fluttered open like butterflies, his dreads swinging.

"This is my seat," I said, pointing to the empty window seat beside him.

He stood up and let me in before sitting back down. He went right back to his position, with his head laid back, eyes closed and air pods in. I studied his features for a moment and noticed that he had a little scar below his right eye, but the rest of his skin was unblemished and the color of strong black coffee with a hint of cream. A masculine jawline accented his face and up top of his head were crinkly dread locks and an edge up that had him looking like he had come straight from the barbershop.

I smiled a little because I automatically started to compare him to

Smoke. They kind of reminded me of one another, just by certain features and their mannerisms. I wondered what Smoke was doing in this very moment. I wondered if he was thinking of me like I was thinking of him. I wondered if he sensed my loneliness like I sensed his anger. Steadily staring at the handsome stranger beside me my thoughts became entangled between him and Smoke. I wondered who the better lover was and why god would place these two men in my path knowing that I couldn't have either of them. I was actually thinking a little ahead of myself, but anything was better than thinking about my reality.

I shook my chaotic thoughts from my head and snuggled up in my blanket, but soon I was looking at him again. Now I wondered what he was listening to that had him so relaxed that he couldn't feel my intense gaze. Like a moth to a flame, his eyes opened, and I tried to turn away quickly so I wouldn't look like a creep and he only smiled, taking one of his air buds out and passing it to me.

So, normally I would not do something that was so unsanitary, but tonight I simply didn't care. I smiled and took the pod and placed it in my ear and I smiled at the sounds of Ari Lenox cooing and before I knew it, I was knocked out.

About eight hours later, we had arrived in Ohio and I slept the entire time, snoring and some more. I stretched before rubbing my belly remembering that I hadn't eaten since the previous morning and I hoped that my cousin would be hospitable and hook me up with some food. I looked over and Stanger was still knocked out. I shook him gently so that I could give him his air pod as the folks started to pile off the bus. He smiled and got up so that we could get our things to go. He grabbed my bags and then his and carried them all.

Once we got off the bus, I could properly stretch as I smiled when the sun hit my skin. The bus had been uncomfortably cold, so sunlight made me happy.

"So—" stranger started.

I turned around to face him and he was just standing there looking at me much like I had done to him last night.

"So.. what?" I said, while grabbing my bag from him.

"I didn't catch your name."

"I didn't give it to you," I said, trying to focus on anything, but him so much that I started to kick up dirt.

"I'm Lex," he said, grabbing a hold of me.

I looked up at his towering frame over me.

"You don't have to me nervous with me," he said, picking up on my nervous pacing.

"I'm not," I said breaking free of his warm touch.

"So, you gone tell me your name or do I have to stand here just looking at your pretty face trying to guess?"

I smiled shyly, never one too big on compliments. "I bet you couldn't guess."

He stored his chin. "You look like an Ashley or a Tiffany."

I chuckled at how far off he was. "Nope, not even close, but I will give you a clue, because it's not that much of a common name. It is closely related to the letter M."

He scratched his head and looked a little confused and I decided just to tell him, though he looked dangerously sexy when he was trying to figure shit out.

"It's Elle."

"Elle?" he repeated.

"Yep, Elle. Like the letter."

"Oh shit, you did say it was closely related to M." He shook his head and laughed.

"ELLE ELLE! Is that you?"

I heard from behind me and though I hadn't seen my cousin in years, I knew her loudmouth from anywhere. I turned around to see her walking up to me her arms stretched wide.

"Heyyy Sherry!" I yelled, matching her enthusiasm.

"Cuzzzzz! I'm so happy that you are here," she said, picking up my bag and pulling me along.

I looked back at Lex and offered him a smile and he nodded. Just that quick he was a stranger again.

FANCY BAPTIST

I massaged Shea butter on my protruding belly after getting out of an hour-long bath. Slipping on a silk two-piece pajama set, I eased to the window to see that Kiyan was still camped out at my house like he had been for the past few nights. A part of me thought that it was sweet, but another part of me thought that it was pathetic.

Kiyan had a way of fucking up and then playing the victim and this time I was not falling into his trap. I did consider taking him back like every day and though I wanted him to, I had to let him sweat for a while. If I let him back in this time, it wouldn't be about just us two, but there would be an entire life added to our equation so he would have to make us a priority in his life.

A part of me rationale with every fuck up that he had ever did, blaming it on his messed-up disorganized childhood. First, he was abandoned by his biological parents and then he went through much more hell all throughout his childhood and adolescence. That was always the main thing that made me take him back when he messed up, but then I learned that he played on that. He knew that I was so empathic to all that he had been through to the point where I made so many excuses for him and he used that to his advantage.

I sat in the sitting area in my bedroom and grabbed my favorite book no matter how many times I read it, *The Notebook*. Don't get me wrong, I loved my urban fiction and my new favorite artist was this new author Named Teshera C, from VA, but my favorite romantic book would always be the notebook. I used to think that the main characters reminded me of Kiyan and I, but boy had those times changed. Kiyan and I had always had a rocky relationship even before we married, but when we first met, he was the sweetest. He chased me for months before I gave him a chance and he was willing to do anything for me Anything.

College days

"Fancy, are you dead ass serious? You're really not going to the party?"

I looked up from my book at my friend who was dressed like she was going to dance on somebody's pole rather that her history class that she had in thirty minutes.

"Are you hard of hearing or just slow? I told you I am not going to that party. I have a test on Monday that I have to pass or I'm going to flunk ,my real estate class."

"Girls, it's Friday! You have the whole damn weekend to study."

"And I have to work, so I'm not going to the party. You are worrying me now girl!" I snapped.

"Girl you are such a party pooper. I bet your man will be there though," she smiled in the mirror causing me to roll my eyes.

"And! We are not Siamese twins you know. He's allowed to go out by himself."

"Well, don't worry friend. I will watch him for you because I'm definitely going to be up in that bitch shaking this ass," she popped her butt up and down making me laugh.

"Well you do that then and trust Kiyan knows better," I boasted.

My roommate Alicia applied another coat of her lipstick to her plump lips and then looked at herself in the mirror.

"Ain't you going to be late for class?" I asked.

"Girl I'm not going to that shit. Its world Lit anyway. Talk about a snooze fest."

I only shook my head at my friend who thought about college more as a party versus a learning experience. Don't get me wrong, I was down to have fun, but I also knew to prioritize.

"But, anyway. I'm out. I'm about to hit the mall to see if I can find something to wear for tonight. Try not to die grandma."

I threw my pillow at her for her not so funny joke. Why did I have to be a grandmother just because I put my scholastics first.

No soon as she walked out, Kiyan was walking in. He looked smooth as hell in his letterman jacket, levi's and fresh wheat Timbs.

"What's up Faye Faye?" he greeted me with a peck on the lips and I could taste the trace of mint on his lips.

"Hey, babe. Where you been?" I asked, right before I noticed that he had a bag of fast food in his hand. He knew that food was the way to my heart.

"You know I have a light load on Friday's, so I been at my room for real," he said, plopping down on my bed beside me. I bit into the burger that he had got me, but I knew that I wouldn't be able to finish it once I felt him planting kisses on my bare legs.

"Uhhh, uhhhh!" I complained. "I have to study."

"Let me help you," he said, steadily kissing my legs and trailing up to my kitty.

"And how is this helping me exactly?" I asked, with a sly smile.

"You have to relax and let me show you," he grabbed the book from my hand and flung it.

I was so hungry that I took one last bite from my burger before I let my man explore my body.

Tugging at my shorts he wasted no time ripping them off before made a face at the sight of my bare kitty.

"Damn bae, you chopped the whole forest down!" he said noticing my fresh razor job.

"Is that going to be a problem?"

He looked up and me and shook his head and smiled before licking his lips and place delicate kissed on my girl. I squirmed in anticipation until he put his entire mouth over my center devouring me whole. I couldn't help but start to pant as he eased one finger inside of me. He peered up to catch my reaction right before my eyes rolled to the back of my head making him suck harder on my throbbing clit.

I lifted my head up a little and started to play with my nipples when I almost jumped out of my skin.

"Oh shit!" I screeched.

Kiyan was so busy nose diving in my seas that he didn't even notice that my roommate Alicia was standing in the doorway just looking at us. I hurriedly yanked Kiyan up and covered myself. I mean Alicia was my roommate but seeing my man and me in the act was something that I was not comfortable with.

"Alicia, what are you doing back?" I asked trying to smooth out my hair.

"Oh, oh," she stuttered. "I forgot my wallet. My bad I didn't mean to bust in on y'all," her eyes then lowered down and when I followed then they were right on Kiyan's exposed dick.

He hurried and threw his jacket over himself.

"But I'ma grab it and go so y'all can get back to doing y'all."

I don't know what it was about her, but she was acting very odd and a part of me wondered how long she had been standing there watching us. She grabbed her wallet and left and as soon as she dotted the door, Kiyan was back all over me, but I was no longer in the mood. The way that my friend was staring at my man had been overthinking now.

–"What's wrong?" he asked after I pushed him off me.

"You didn't peep that?" I asked.

"Peep what?" he asked dumbfounded. Dudes were so blind sometimes at things that were right in their faces.

"Nothing," I said, getting up.

"Yo, did I do something? I'm confused," he said, and I sensed his tone.

"I'm just not in the mood anymore."

"Well WE are," he said, pointing to his dick that was still brick hard.

Without even giving him a response, I walked to the bathroom to clean myself up and when I came back out, Kiyan was putting his clothes on and I could tell that he was mad just by the way he was rushing so that he could leave.

"Are you mad?" I asked.

"Faye, what the fuck am I supposed to be?"

"Not mad because I'm not in the mood to have sex like we don't do it all the time! You act like you are deprived out here or something."

"That is what it feels like sometimes."

"UNBELIVABLE!" I said throwing my hands up in frustration.

He walked by me to leave without so much as a fuck you.

"Have fun tonight," I said, sarcastically.

"No doubt, and uhh don't wait up," he smirked like he was threatening me or something.

After he left, I hit the books again, but instantly fell asleep. When I woke up the night had fallen, and the clock read ten pm. I checked my phone, but I had not missed calls or texts letting me know that Kiyan was still playing mad. I called his phone and just like I thought he didn't answer.

I got back to studying, but my mind wasn't focused on shit that was in a book. I wanted to make up with Kiyan so that we could get back to being our lovey dovey selves. I called his phone once more and again he didn't answer sending me straight to voice mail.

After going back in forth in my mind, I decided that I would show up to this party. I showered and got dressed within an hour and I looked good if I didn't say so myself. The leather mini skirt that I wore clung to my curves and I paired it with a colorful Coogi sweater and biker jacket. On my feet were length knee high boot and I styled my hair in the half up half dawn look. Spraying my Velvet petal body mist on my neck and wrists, I did one final look in the mirror before dashing out of the door.

I made it to the location of the party which was at an off-campus apartment and from the outside, I knew that the party was jumpin'. Cars were lined up on both sides of the street and some were even blocking people's driveways. I walked up to the packed porch with guys smoking weed and girls laughing at their corny jokes all in an effort to be down. Bypassing them, I made it into the house which was crowed from wall to wall. The music was blasting, and everyone had red cups in their hand. I spotted Daryl, Kiyan's home boy and approached him.

"Hey where is your friend?"

He froze for a moment and then tried to play it off, but I had already caught it.

"That man somewhere around here," he as he typed away on his phone.

"Oh okay," I said, not really trying to press the issue. I would just find him myself.

I walked through the dancing sweaty bodies in hope of finding my boyfriend but had no such luck.

Finally, deciding that I would just see him in the morning. I made my way outside to my car when I spotted Alicia's car, it was a few cars down from mine and I wondered why I hadn't seen her inside. I walked over to her car and the windows were a little fogged up like she was smoking or something. I knocked on her window and I could see the silhouette of two bodies. This girl was really getting freaky in the car. I was just about to walk away when I noticed whoever it was had on a light blue sweater, much like the one that Kiyan was wearing earlier.

Trying my luck, I opened the door and there my friend was, curled up in the back seat with my boyfriend getting her back blown out. It took the two a minute to register that they had been caught, but they were a minute too slow as I leapt into the back seat like a wild woman. Grabbing Alicia's hair, I banged her head to the back widow until I started to see blood.

"Faye, come on man let her go. It's not what it looks like," I heard Kiyan say.

"Ahhhh get off of me! Kiyan get her off me," Alicia whined.

Kiyan finally managed to pull me off Alicia and next I was wilding on his ass. I didn't care where my punches landed as long as they were on him.

"Calm the fuck down," he said once he finally got me outside of the car.

"You cheating dog!" I yelled out before gawking a glob of spit on him. Yeah, it was nasty, but he deserved it.

By then Alicia had sped off, but the bitch had better find another place to live because I was going to be on her ass every time, I saw her.

"Faye, STOP!" Kiyan demanded wiping his face and grabbing my hand to stop me from going crazy.

"Get the hell off me. Go follow your whore!" I yelled, trying to break free from him, but it wasn't working. I was not match for the all-star athlete.

Calming down, I looked him dead in his eyes wondering how he could do what he did to me and with my friend at that.

"Look, I'm sorry Faye. That shit was foul but," he started.

"BUT! There is no but! You slept with my friend and now you are out here looking at me in my face like I'm stupid."

Kiyan just looked down and shook his head and I grabbed away from him and ran to my car. He chased me down, but he must have tripped over something because when he finally got to me, I was driving off. When I made it to my room Alicia's side was cleared out like she had grabbed all of her things and left. The bitch was smarter than I thought.

For the next couple of weeks, I ignored Kiyan. He would show up to my dorm every day, with his lies and I wouldn't even give him the time of the day. He even showed up at my classes, but I ignore him just like he was Casper the friendly ghost. In my mind I was done with Kiyan. I was too young to sit and let a boy play me like there were no other fish in the sea.

One day while I was locking up the financial aid office that I did work study at, Kiyan came just as I had the key in the door and pushed me back in shutting the door behind us.

"KIYAN!" I yelled.

He put his hand up to silence me. "Look, just hear me out. I fucked up Faye. I really fucked up and I would do anything to make it right between us. Please just tell me what I have to do," he pleaded.

I had never seen him cry or be so apologetic and it seemed sincere, but there was only one thing and one thing only that needed to be done.

"Kill her," I said with no emotion at all.

Kiyan looked at me with the screw face probably trying to figure out if I was serious or not.

"That's what you have to do," I said, breezing past him leaving the decision up to him.

I got up going back to the window, and Kiyan was gone.

PIA KENNEDY

⚜

I made my way up to the jail secretly happy that I would be able to see my man. Lord knows I missed him and even though these visits were short lived, just being in his presence got me by these days. After going through the extensive search and with the guards AKA the welcoming committee, I was finally in the waiting room with the rest of the girlfriends, wives and family, waiting.

I took my compact mirror out, making sure that my lip gloss was on point and trailing my eyebrows when I looked up at some inmate staring me down. He looked like he could have belonged to the group bone Wu-Tang Clan with the several tattoos that ran down his face and the scowl that he wore on his face. The shit was kind of scary, so I turned to the other side of the table only to catch another weird looking person in my face. I had to remind myself that these deprived men were in jail and would lust after anything in a skirt.

After, ten minutes of waiting, I spotted Flame strutting over. Baby boy was getting a little buff from being locked up and by now I'm pretty sure his newfound muscles matched his big ass ego. I smiled and extended my arms when he walked up, but he only looked stone faced. He then looked me up a down followed by him just sitting down without saying a word.

"Heyyyy!" I said, excitedly scooting a little closer to him.

"What's up?" was the only thing he said.

I didn't know what was going on with him, but his entire vibe was throwing me off.

"Soo, how are you?" I asked, still trying to be positive and not ruin the visit.

"Yo, put your fucking feet under the table," he motioned for me to move my feet.

I looked down at my feet and wondered what he was talking about. I placed my white coted toenails under the table and then turned my attention back to him.

"Why are my feet being out bothering you?"

"Why the fuck do you got that shit on? You came here to see me, not play dress up and put on a damn show," he said quietly, but still with enough force to make the hair on my arms stand up.

I looked down at the basic outfit that I had on which consisted of a pencil skirt and a ruffled top and open toed pumps. I called myself trying to be causally cute for my man and here he was complaining because I was getting more attention than him. Typical Flame.

"Well, I try to look decent for you, but maybe I would be better if I just wore, t-shirts and sweats."

"Yeah you do that. When niggas cheesing and looking all goofy at my girl, it never ends well," he said, confidently.

I only rolled my eyes up to the sky ready to just get up and leave.

"Keep rolling them, and them shits gone get stuck like that," I heard him say.

"So, is this what we gone do for the whole visit. Do I have to listen to you bitch the entire time?" I asked, fed up with his attitude.

"It's whatever you want to do," he folded his arms like he wasn't about to be the first one to backdown, but luckily, I wasn't as childish as he was.

"So, what's new? Have you heard anything from Kiyan?" I asked referring to his case.

"Yeah, shit getting handled," he said, shortly.

"Okay, so that is good," I said, getting back perked up.

Still, Flame's mood hadn't changed and I knew he couldn't have been this mad because other men were looking at me. I did know him to be the jealous type, but I wasn't checking for any of these men, let alone men who were in the same position that he was in.

I let out a sigh and shook my head.

"Problem?" he asked.

I chuckled. "You know what, I do have a problem," I said staring up at the ceiling before my gaze finally met him.

"Enlighten me," he said, with his hand clasped together.

"Okay cool," I said, with a slick smile. "My problem is that I waste my time fucking with one nigga when I should be dating seven, hell ten! My problem is I can't figure out for the life of me why I always get so entangled in these weak ass relationships when I really just need to be free to fuck with and just fuck whoever I want to. That's my problem," I said, returning his arrogance.

He smirked. "P, it isn't gone be hospital that can fix that slick ass mouth if you don't tread lightly."

I could tell that Flame was on fire as his jaw was clenched and his temple was beaming from the side of his head., I grabbed my purse and stormed out. Flame had ruined my mood and I wasn't going to continue to sit in his face while he was trying to treat a bitch.

I got in my car and drove away from the jail like a bat out of hell. I had no intention of returning ever and Flame had better not think of dialing my line. Before him, I was out enjoying my life and I would continue to do the same after him. I was driving so fast and cursing Flame out along the way that I was not paying attention to the road and I slammed into the back of someone's G-wagon.

I stopped hard on my breaks, but by them it was too late, and I saw the driver's door being swung open. Today was just not my damn day. I jumped out of my car ready to apologize profusely and give the person my insurance information, but all of that went out of the window very quickly.

"Damn bitch fuck you get your license from? Look at my fucking car!" the driver snapped.

I said a silent prayer in my head so that I could hold my composure, but if one more bitch came out of his mouth, I was going to hit his ass with my car next.

"Fuck you standing over there looking dumb for? Do you see my fucking car," he continued to go on.

"Look, here is my insurance info, all of that is not necessary," I said, referring to all the crying that he was doing.

He ignored my comment and got on his phone and proceeded to tell someone that he had just got into an accident. He was going on and on like a little bitch.

"Umm excuse me, it's hot out here and I don't have time to stand out here with you all day. Are you going to take the info or no?"

Just then a seven series matte black BMW pulled alongside of us and I suddenly felt nervous. Flame had always reminded me to take my taser out with me and my hard-headed ass never listened. Now here I was with one crazy person and possibly another one had just pulled up.

I grabbed my keys quickly remembering that I had pepper spray on my key ring, and I prepared to use it. I just hoped that some crazy shit wasn't about to go down all because I had rear ended someone. I braced myself and held my finger steady on the pepper spray when the person who was in the car finally stepped out.

"Bruh, look at this shit," the other one went on. "Her dumb ass ran into me at a fucking red light," he pointed to me and rolled his eyes.

"YO CHILL OUT!" the other man finally spoke, and he had my full attention from his butter pecan colored skin to his to the way he commanded attention just by the tone of his voice.

The other man tried to go on, but he quickly stopped noticing the look on the other one's face. The guy walked around and inspected the damages to the car without saying a word, while the other stupid one sulked.

"Um, hi I'm sooo sorry to inconvenience you and your friend's time like this. My insurance will cover the damages," I said, handing him my insurance card so that he could take a picture of it.

For the first time since he stepped on the scene, he looked up at me and his eyes lingered for a moment. I took in his big brown eyes and handsome looks and I had to look away quickly.

"You good. Shit happens," he said, with a shrug. "This is only one of my cars."

"Ohh this is your car? Not his?" I pointed to his mad friend.

"Nah, this fool was supposed to been taking it to my detailing shop for me and he was out joy riding. The shop way on the other side of town. How you get all the way over here?" he was now talking to the other dude.

"Ri, it's not even like that man. I was just handling some business," he spoke.

It was so funny how he was just popping so much shit before and now he was stuttering like a kid was being scolded by his daddy. I couldn't help but laugh.

"So, where you were rushing off to, looking like that?" Ri turned his attention to me, looking me up and down.

"I was on my way to the nearest bar to drink my problems away, but god had other plans."

"You still trying to do that?"

"Do what?"

"Get some drinks."

"I just hit your car and you are asking me about drinks," I laughed. "Absolutely not. After the day I had. All I want is my bed and to be left alone."

"Shit, this little dent," he pointed. "I can have that shit fixed by tomorrow. I'm not even sweating it, but you enjoy your night miss lady," he said, in this sexy low tone that made my knees buckle.

"You don't want to contact my insurance?" I asked.

"Nah, ain't no need for all of that. I will see you around though." With that he walked away instructing his friend to drive the g-wagon and he hoped back in his BMW.

I got back into my car after seeing that the front of my car only had a few scratches that a fresh ain't job could fix. I drove home and a smile couldn't help but form on my face thinking about the charming man that I had just met. I didn't know what was in the cards for Flame and me, but tonight I had someone else to think about.

KIYAN BAPTIST

I did my morning rounds at the hospital and ended up staying longer than I expected. There was always some hatting or something unexpected happening with a patient that made my shifts hours long than they were supposed to be. I exited the hospital with only two places in my mind, to get tome grub and then heading straight home to get in the bed.

I walked into the local pastry shop, my mouth set on having a strawberry cheesecake scone and a black cup of coffee.

"What's up big dog?" I greeted the owner. This little shop wasn't far from the hospital so I supported whenever I could, and it was black owned.

"My guy," Hector extended his hand to shake mine.

I ordered my things and talked with Hector for a while just catching up on the things that I had missed within the last few weeks since I had last visited.

"And man wasn't that crazy how Pops just died like that? That was my brother from another mother," Hector stroked is bald head. The pained look on his face was apparent. He really missed his friend.

"Yeah, that shit got to me, you know pops was the closet to a father figure that I ever had. I really messed me up that I wasn't able to say goodbye," I shook my head.

"Man, and ain't it crazy that I was just as I was going to the hospital. I saw his daughter leaving out. When I got up there to see him, I saw that no one could go in his room and then fifteen minutes later, they were saying that he was dead. I didn't know what to do man," Hector went on.

As I half listened to him go on, my mind was stuck on hearing that Sandy had been leaving the hospital while her father was dying. That shit was odd because Hector never mentioned her coming back and no-one else had ever mentioned that Sandy had even been there visiting her father before he died. I couldn't put my finger on it, but something smelled fishy.

"Well, Hec, I'm going to get out of here. You enjoy the rest of your day old man," I rested my hand on his shoulder and he smiled a warmly.

"And you be good youngin' and send Fancy my love."

I turned to walk away and was met with the eyes of a stranger. I smiled and tried to walk around her, but she stopped me.

"So, you are a doctor?" she randomly asked.

"Excuse me," I commented.

"Oh, I'm sorry," the older woman laughed bashfully. "I met you briefly the other day. You know, your wife was showing me the house."

"Ohhhh, forgive me. I couldn't place your face," I joked.

There was a moment of silence between the two of us and she just stared making me a little nervous. Her gaze was so powerful.

"Well, you enjoy your day," I said, trying to break away from her hold.

"Can I ask you something?" she finally spoke up.

"Sure."

"Would you mind just sitting with an old lady. I know that you may be busy and all, but—" the words trailed off as she looked away. She seemed embarrassed by her own request, but I couldn't just blow this sweet woman off no matter no tired I was.

"I can do that," I smiled escorting her to a nearby table. She ordered coffee and a bagel, and we talked for about an hour. She stated that she had just lost a son and a daughter and how I reminded her of him from the first day that she had seen me so she had to stop me.

Yeah, she seemed a little strange at first, but after getting to know her, I learned that she was just lonely and needed some company.

I made it home finally and I was surprised to see that Fancy's car was in the driveway. I hope that she wasn't coming with no bullshit because I was tired out of my mind and just didn't have time for the dramatics. I walked into my home and I was immediately hit with the scent of some soulful cooking in the kitchen. It was Sunday and Fancy usually cooked a big meal on Sunday's, but I hadn't experienced that in forever.

I walked in the kitchen and peeped my head in the oven to see baked macaroni and yams cooking. I rubbed my hands together as I could already taste Fancy's southern skills on my tongue. Cooking was just one of Fancy's many talents that I had taken for granted. I peeped my head in the fridge and grabbed a bottle of water and when I closed it, Fancy was just standing there.

"Boo," she said, without much enthusiasm at all, but it still scared me.

"Damn girl, you can't be sneaking up on folks like that."

"Do I scare you?" she asked, with a sadistic smile.

"A little."

She smiled. "So, lets chat," she purred me a glass of wine even though it was only two pm and I had just worked an overnight shift. I looked at her like she was crazy when she started to pour herself a glass.

"Calm down, the doctor said one glass is fine," she attempted to take a sip, but I snatched it from her grip.

"I'm your doctor, now what on your mind?"

"So, I'm willing to give this another chance; us another chance," she started.

I perked up at her mention of us getting back together. She didn't know how badly I wanted this, how badly I wanted her.

"But under one condition. There will be no bullshit this go around," she walked to the drawer where I the knives were housed and grabbed the biggest butcher knife that she could find. Walking back over to be with a sultry strut and that same sick ass smile on her face.

She twirled the knife, "There will be blood, preferably yours if you screw me over this time Kiyan," her tone was so calm compared to the look in her eyes that it was scary.

She walked a little closer to me with the knife and started to poke at my chest with it. My eyes never left her and she poked me with the knife deeper and deeper until she saw the crimson colored blood started to seep through my light blue scrubs.

"You understand?" she asked, unfazed.

I grabbed the knife from her even more unfazed by her little threats.

"So, go and shower, the food should be ready in about an hour," she turned away and went to the oven. Her voice was no longer laced with venom and it was like she had turned into a different person just that quickly. All I could do was shake my head, knowing that Fancy had always had a dark side to her that not many had seen or would ever want to see. She was the Yin to my Yang.

FLAME BAPTIST

"Man, not today, I don't have time for this shit," I said, as soon as I walked into the room and spotted Stephany Bianchi.

My girl had just walked out on me from a visit and right now I wanted to ring somebody's neck. I didn't know how badly I enjoyed setting nigga's ablaze until I came up in this bitch. I needed to let off some major steam and the only way that I could do that was being in something tight and wet or to light some shit up.

Pia was really on some carrying me type shit. First, she walked up into this bitch like I t was a fashion show or something then she called herself treating a nigga. I don't know if our foundation wasn't strong enough yet, but I was definitely questioning shit between us. Lately, we had been arguing about little shit and even though we would get past it, I had a feeling that Pia wasn't about this holding a nigga down life.

Oh, and that mouth was off the chain. Shorty was talking reckless to a nigga like I was average or one of the lame ass niggas that she used to fuck with. It was eating me up that she was just able to talk shit and leave, but to be honest I couldn't even focus on that shit. I needed to be a free man ad my freedom was more important than going back and forth with Pia. I'm sure her tune would change anyways once I was on the streets again.

"Yo', we not doing this," I warned Stephany. "I didn't even know that she was here."

"Look Kindal, just here me out. What if I said, I could get you out within the next week?"

I perked up a little hearing her say that sitting down in the chair across from her, but I played it cool.

"Talk," I demanded.

"First, I need to know if you did it or not."

"Did what?" I played dumb.

"Did you set the fire that killed your foster parents eight years ago?" she asked blatantly.

I sat up in my chair and looked at her dead in her eyes. And smiled. "No," I lied.

No matter if she thought that she was my lawyer or not, I would never admit shit to anybody about anything that I had ever did. She could make assumptions in her head all that's she wanted, but she wouldn't ever get shit from me.

"Okay, now that we got that out of the way," she said, unmoved. I knew that she wasn't believing shit that I was feeding her.

"So, I have a way to get my hands on that recording, but I need you to be honest with me and let me know if there is anything that I need to know about. Anything that you think that may come up from your past that will try to be used against you."

"You said you did your research right? I'm an open book. Muggs bitch ass gone try to pin anything and everything on me, but truth be told I am the owner of barbershop, nothing more nothing less," I said, confidently.

Stephany stared at me for a moment as she shifted in her seat. I could've sworn I saw her lick her lips too and I only smiled. She didn't want these big dick problems in her life, so she better had gotten that look off of her face.

"Okay, so here is the deal," she said, crossing her legs. "Let me talk to my connect and make some moves and I WILL have you out of here with in a few days, but let's make one thing clear, I'm not doing this for my health. Are you on my retainer or no?"

"For now, My brother can hit you with some dough, but you have exactly one week and if I don't see any results, you may as well carry your ass back to the crack den where you came from."

Stephany laughed. "Are you always this nice to the people who are trying to help you?"

"Less questions and more action," I said, getting up from the table.

Stephany's eyes roamed my toned body before they fell on my dick print. Baby girl wasn't even trying to hide it by the way she bit her lips. When she finally stood, I got a peek at her too and I could tell that she was packing under the suit that she was wearing. He titties tried tough her button up and her ass threatened to rip the burgundy slacks that she was wearing. I couldn't help but chuckle while trying to shake the nasty thought from my head. A nigga hadn't had any action in damn a while so I would punish anything walking at this point.

"I'll be seeing you Mr. Baptist." My last name rolled off her tongue, laced with her Italian accent. Still no matter how sexy she tried to be, my dick only got hard for one hardheaded ass talking female and that was Pia.

SMOKE BAPTIST

I sat in the back of the dimly lit restaurant scoping out the scene waiting for my guests to arrive. Right now, a thick ass broad was in my view and I could tell she was gaming the nigga that she was with. She kept reaching her hand under the table and each time the man would smile this lazy grin. She looked half his age from his receding hair line to the silk shirt that he wore and greasy ass lips.

I chuckled under my breath, feeling a little sorry for the man. I could spot a sack chaser from a mile away and this one was definitely it. She wasn't bad on the eyes either, her light unblemished skin, long blonde weave and red dress that I could tell would creep up her ass as soon as she stood, proved that she was bleed him dry tonight. Females like her weren't after anything, but the loot and I just hoped for the dude that the nut was worth how dry she was about to run his pockets.

Taking my attention from them, I glanced at the front entrance and in walked Muggs and her partner Spence. I could not stand his cracker ass either, but he wasn't as bad as Muggs. He just had a following problem. Whatever she told him; he went for like a little bitch. That type of boy deserved o respect.

"So, what is up Muggs. Why did you drag me out knowing that I have a date tonight?" Spence asked once they were sitting.

"Damn straight to it huh?" Muggs replied. "Well, I have an opportunity for you."

Spence shook his head a and chuckled a bit. "And let me guess, it involves the Baptist brothers doesn't it ? Why do you have such a hard on for those guys?"

Muggs leaned back in her chair, " I just need those filthy animals off the streets. One of them tried to rape me and my own father didn't even believe me I already have one and now I just need the other three."

She was really laying it on thick. I shook my head at how Muggs would stop at nothing to have my brothers and me. This bitch had been trying to bring us down for years and she was still trying.

"So, what is this opportunity that you speak of?" Spence asked. He seemed like he was all in for the bullshit that she was about to present.

Looking around before she spoke, Muggs leaned over and whispered in his ear as if she knew that I was watching her. She whispered to him briefly before a smile appeared on his face. Once she leaned back over Spence only nodded.

Damn, I wished like hell that I knew what she had said to him. My main reason for being here tonight was to see if she had any information on where Elle could be, but at this point she was not really giving me shit. Muggs was smart in that ay though, she always tied up all her lose ends and she made sure to watch her back.

"So how have you been with the death of your father?" Spence asked changing the topic.

"Ehh, you know him and I weren't really close."

"Damn so y'all didn't make up at all before he died?"

"Nope," she said, shortly.

"What were you guy's issue, everyone loved him and respected him, but you."

"That man was a fraud and thank god he's no longer here to spread his fraudulence," Muggs said cockily.

I couldn't help but shake my head at the disdain that she had for her father who never did anything but try and help her. She always rebelled and was out doing fuck shit and I was not the smartest in the world, but any blind person could see that something was wrong with her. She was a little off and Pops refused to believe that shit thinking that she was just acting out because she didn't have a motherly figure in her life.

"You are one crazy son of a gun," Spence said with a chuckle, but I could tell that he was kind of thrown off in the way that Muggs spoke about her dad. "I'm going to go ahead and get out of here. I have some nice ass waiting on me, but I will see you tomorrow at the office," I laughed at his white wacky ass.

"Okay and think on what I said," she said, right before he smiled and walked away.

Not even five minutes after he walked away in walked another dude and to my surprise, he walked up to her and placed a nasty kiss on her lips that left her smiling after. By now I for sure thought that she was playing for the other team so to see her live in the flesh with another man almost made me hurl. Any nigga that was interested in Muggs must've lost or bet or had an intellectual disability.

The two sat down to talk and I thought that this would be the perfect time to make my presence known. I got up from the table that Muggs had never noticed me at and walked over to her and took a seat.

"Sandy," I said, looking at the mean mug that was now on her face. I smiled, taking a bite of the bread that was on her table pissing her off even more. I didn't even acknowledge her nigga or whoever he was supposed to be.

"What the lick read?" I followed up.

"I'm not aware of your gangster lingo, but you need to get up from this table and leave NOW!" her deranged ass called herself snapping.

"Or what? You gone try to pin some bogus ass shit on me or one of my brothers, or better yet you gone try to say I raped you.. again," I chuckled.

"Yo', fuck is this nigga?" the dude she was sitting with finally spoke up.

"Oh, you don't me? That's weird. I'm the nigga whose dick yo' bitch wish she was sucking," I sat back calmly as the dude got up like he was about to do something.

"Baby, calm down," Muggs tried calming him.

"Yeah. Tell him to sit his bitch ass down. You and I can talk man to man."

"I'm going to nail your bitch ass. You think I don't know what you and your brothers have been up to around this town? When I'm done with all of you, you will be rooting," she said, with a cocky grin. The teeth in her mouth were still just as stained and crooked.

"Yeah, we are not even about to discuss your empty threats. That's not what I'm here for."

"Patna, whatever type of business you got going on with her you better make it fast because I'm starting to lose patience," dude spoke up again.

I paid him no mind and kept my attention on Muggs. "Where is Elle?" I didn't even have to go into nothing else because I already knew that Muggs knew her.

A lazy grin spread across her face and I couldn't help but smirk at her left eye which was always a little more hooded than the other earning her the name left eye when we were younger.

"This is too funny, You come interrupting my dinner because you are worried about your little raggedy ass bitch," she was the one chuckling now. "You're asking me where she is, how would I know?"

"Let's be serious, anything regarding me, you definitely know so come on. Entertain me."

"Even if I knew I wouldn't tell you shit about your little girlfriend's where abouts, but what I will say is she put the nail in Kindal's coffin, so if I were you I would watch the pillow talk," she said, with a smirk.

"Let's go ," she said, to her puppet before she got up to leave. I didn't know what to do with the info that she had called herself giving me, and the shit just made me even more confused, but now more than ever I knew that I had to find Elle.

"Bye Left Eye!" I yelled out and she shot me with the death stare prompting me to blow her a kiss.

While walking out, dude looked back at me and for a moment he just started like he was trying to figure me out or something. Never being the one to back down, I returned his menacing glare trying to find something familiar about him, but I couldn't. He broke the staring contest and then followed behind his bulldog and once again I was left with more questions.

SCAR BANKS

I sat inside of the cold waiting room waiting for my baby brother to come out. I hated visiting Jail and if it wasn't for the love that I had for my younger brother Jacob, I would never be in this bitch. I had done a four-year bid and I promised myself that I would never come back. I would rather be carried by six than to be judged by twelve.

-- I glanced at the expensive diamond encrusted watch that adorned my wrist noticing that I had been sitting in this fucking waiting room for over thirty minutes, just waiting. I was a very impatient man, something that I had tried to work on over the years unsuccessfully. My once rested hands started to tap on the table, and I looked around daring someone to stop me.

Another ten minutes passed and just as I was about to go and talk to someone about it, out walked my baby brother. He looked bad. He was always a scrawny little kid, but now he looked like her had lost mad weight and the expression on his face let me know that he was not doing so well. Once he looked up, he saw me and his sorrowful look disappeared and turning into a full-fledged smile.

I got up to hugged him and I held him tightly, but not too long because I knew that the guards would start to bitch.

"What's up with you baby boy?" I asked, grabbing a hold of the back of his head. Jacob was not only my little brother, but my best friend and it killed me to see him locked up like some animal when he was nowhere near animal like. Now me on the other hand, I was a beast I did my crime and my time easily, but my brother he didn't belong here.

"I'm trying to make it man," he answered me.

I gave him the snacks that I had purchase him and he immediately started to open them gobbling them down like he hadn't ate in weeks.

"Chill out boy, it's not going anywhere," I joked.

"I know man, I'm just hungry, that's all," he said, with his head down and I could tell that there was something that he was not telling me.

"What been going on in here man and be honest with me."

"Nothing," he lied.

"Come on man, how am I supposed to help you if I don't know what's going on," I preached.

My brother remained quiet as if he had to, like he was scared to tell me the truth and that shit pissed me off even more, but I knew that I couldn't push him. He was already weak and I didn't want to break him.

"Look bruh, you know I'm working on shit on the outside. I'm going to get you out of here, but I will have to take things into my own hands."

Jacob looked at me with fear in his eyes. "Please don't, just let the lawyers handle it. I don't want you to get in trouble too. We both can't be in here."

It's crazy because Jacob had been in jail for since he was a Junior in high school and now at nineteen, it was like he hadn't grown developmentally since the day he had walked into this bitch. Me being his big brother, the only thing I wanted to do was protect him since we were kids and now, I felt like I was letting him down. I had managed to get locked up and he got involved with a bitch who was his downfall.

"Jacob, I have to do something. You know I'm your big brother and

I got you. You must trust in me though. Trust that I'm not going to let you down."

Jacob looked up his mouth filled with Oreos. "You know I always wanted to be like you right? From the way you dressed to the way that all the girls flocked to you. I always admired my big brother and knew that you would always protect me. That stands true to this day, I know that you will always be here for me." He looked like he was about to tear up.

"Don't start that shit Jacob," I joked. "Nigga always have to make shit a moment."

I pulled him closer to me and we embraced. I was going to get my brother out if was the last thing that I did and if there was a little blood shed while doing it then so be it.

STEPHANY BIANCHI

"That's right! Get down on your fucking knees!" I said, as I kicked my sub down to his knees. He tried to say something, but I just hushed him and my foot of my boot in his mouth. His labored breathing was full on panting now as I looked down on him.

"What are you going to do for mam?" I asked him, yanking at the dog collar that was around his neck.

"What, whatever mama wants me to do," he stuttered.

"Anything?" I repeated

"Yes, anything mama."

"On your feet!" I demanded and he hopped up, his hand still tied behind his back.

"What do you want me to do to you tonight?"

"I want you to make me your bitch," he said, confidently and I only laughed. For as long as I had known Spence, he had been into BDSM and with each time we got together his fantasy became more and more twisted. Last month he wanted me to me to treat him like a fairy and tonight he wanted me to be my bitch. Spence was laughable, but more than that he was an asset.

"Down," I commanded, and he dropped to his knees again.

"Come."

I began to walk out of the room and he followed still on his knees. I escorted him down to the lower level of his home which he had converted into a sex dungeon. Anything you could name was there from penis bands to butt plugs.

"Mama is going to make you a little bitch, but I need you to do something for me. Lay down."

I uncuffed him and he hopped up on the table that was coated in leather and laid flat on his stomach. I grabbed the leather whip from the wall that was filled with various whip and gently rubbed it across his back. He jumped at first when the cold leather his back and then he started to relax bit slumping his shoulders.

I raised the whip up and then brought it down hard on his ass making him shriek. I hit him once more causing him to holler.

"You want me to stop?" I asked, loudly knowing he didn't.

"No, mama please don't stop," he said, breathlessly.

I started to see the red welts form on his skin as he wiggled in anticipation. Deciding to speed the party up a notch. I grabbed the anal spark plug and teased his botty hole with it. This nigga was howling out and it wasn't even in yet.

"Please mama put it in. Put it in," he begged, but I decided to make him wait a little.

"Mama needs you to make something disappear," I said, circling around his hole with the plug. The vibration was getting to him in a good way.

"There is a little recording floating around your precinct that I need gone. I need all traces of it to disperse. Do you understand mama?" I asked, finally inserting the plug, but only about an inch or so.

"Mama, I am your bitch. Whatever you want me to do I will."

That got me excited as I positioned the plug further and further inside of his anus. Spence took it like a pro squeezing his buttocks together and letting out bitch like moans.

For the rest of the night I entertained my BDSM sub knowing that soon my client would be out of jail and my pockets would be a helluvuh lot fatter.

ELLE LONDON

It was my second day being at my Cousin's in Ohio and I was still getting settled in. My cousin was doing good for herself. She had a nice luxury apartment and was holding it down as a dental hygienist. I knew my cousin wondered what brought be to Ohio so abruptly, but she opened her home to me without asking any questions and she assured me that I could stay as long as I needed to.

I sat at her kitchen Island eating a bowl of Lucky Charms when she walked in.

"Hey cuz," she greeted me. She had on white scrubs so I'm guessing that she was just coming in from work.

"Hey girl," I said, dryly partly because I had so much on my mind and my heart.

"What's wrong with you?" she asked, picking up on my mood.

"Nothing, just thinking."

"Well, let me in then. You know I would never judge you because we all done been through shit cuz."

Still not wanting to divulge too much of my personal life, I opted to continue to lie.

"I'm fine cousin, really. I just need to get some rest."

"Get some rest? You been sleeping since you got here. What you need is a day of fun."

"Ohhh, no you don't. don't go planning stuff in your head for me to do. I am fine being in the house."

"Come on Cuz, Summer is almost over. And you need to have some fun. Live a little."

"Sherry, trust I've lived and that probably why I am in the predicament that I am in now," I said, solemnly.

Sherry wore a look or pity mixed with concern on her face.

Just then there was a knock on the door. Sherry gently squeezed my hand before going to answer it.

"Who is it?" she yelled, and I head a male voice, but I didn't hear what he said his name was.

Sherry came walking back into the kitchen about twenty seconds later with a grin on her face.

"It's for you."

I turned my nose up knowing that she had to be joking. "Quit playing girl."

"I'm not. The door is for you now get your butt up and see who it is."

Panic suddenly started to set in for me thinking that it was Smoke or Muggs. I'm not sure how they would have found me, but now I had to face what I had coming. I slowly rose from the chair flattened out my hair that was on the top of my head. Sherry stood there smiling and she didn't even know that I was about to piss on myself.

I nervously walked to the door and I was met with a surprise. It was Lex.

He noticed the look on my face and smiled.

"Weird right? but I think I made a mistake and took your phone. You didn't notice that it was missing?" he asked in his sultry baritone voice.

I had only been here for two days and come to think of it, I hadn't even realized that I didn't have my phone because I didn't use it much these days. It was a little corner store phone anyway because I had got rid of my old one just in case someone tried to track it.

"So, it was a mistake that you took my phone?" I asked, as he handed it to me.

"You are welcome and yes it was a mistake. I tried to reach out to your most recent contacts, but you didn't have any numbers saved. I looked in your maps and this this was the last Ohio address that was searched so I just decided to bring it here."

"You did an awful lot to bring me this track phone."

"Yeah, I did, and I wanted to bring it to you personally."

I stared at him for a moment and tried to read him, but I got nothing and then I remembered how I looked at the time. I crossed my arms over my chest and removed the reading glasses that I had on. I looked a mess in a hot pink robe, fuzzy socks and a messy bun.

Lex smirked at me trying to fix myself.

"Is that all?" I asked.

"Do you want it to be?"

"I don't know what I want to be honest," I looked down at my socks. "But thank you for returning my phone."

"UMM LEX IS IT? WOULD YOU LIKE TO STAY FOR DINNER?" I heard my loud ass cousin yell from the kitchen and Lex and I instantly started to laugh.

"UHH!" he yelled out contemplating the idea.

"You mind?" he asked me lowly. "You know I didn't track you down just to bring you your phone back," he smiled handsomely.

"Now, I'm starting to think you took it on purpose, but it's cool, my cousin and I would love to have you for dinner, as long as you are not a serial killer or an axe murderer."

He put his hand up in the air. "Aye, I'm a good guy."

"Okay, you better be. But you can make yourself comfortable in the living room. I will be back down in a few," I headed up the stairs so that I could freshen up and put on some decent clothes.

I came back down about thirty minutes later in a Juicy Couture sweat suit and I put a little heat to my hair, so it fell straight sown my back with a middle part.

"'Bout time, thickums," Sherry said, when I came down. I looked down at spreading thighs and chuckled. Gone were the days when I was in a size two because now, I was wearing at least a seven.

"So Elle, I have to make a run really quick. You can take the food out of the oven in about twenty minutes and if I'm not back by then y'all can go ahead and eat without me," she tried creeping up the stairs, but I followed her.

"Girl, you think that you are so slick, You are not about to leave me here with this man who you invited to stay for dinner."

"Girl you will be fine. There are plenty of knives around this bitch. Live a little and just chill and have some adult conversation. You been sitting around here looking like you lost your best friend. Just enjoy this man who obviously likes you for an hour or two."

I pouted a little right before she grabbed her keys and whizzed by me. After she left, I stayed upstairs for an additional twenty minutes hoping that Lex would just leave, but when I emerged down the stairs he was taking the food out of the oven.

"I see you've made yourself at home?" I stated.

"Well, I couldn't let the house burn down," he said, sarcastically.

I grabbed a glass and poured myself a glass of red wine.

"So, you really going to sit there and let me do all of the work in your house?" he chuckled.

"Yep, and you are doing perfect so far."

I watched him as he looked through the cabinet for the plates and little did he know, but I was just as clueless as he was being that I had just moved here. He finally found them and then he started to plate the food, which was five cheese Lasagna, salad and garlic bread.

Once he made the plates, he sat down and I was about to dig right in, but he grabbed my hand and started to bless the food. Once he finished, we both started to eat in silence as there was a little awkwardness that lingered in the air.

"Soooo," he started.

"Soooo," I repeated and we both started to laugh.

"What is your story?" he finally asked once we got back serious.

"Well, there is not much to tell, so what would you like to know?"

"Where are you from originally and wat brought you here?"

"I'm originally from North Carolina and I'm here because I just needed a fresh start."

"I guess you can say the same for me too, but in a strange way I feel like you and I meeting was supposed to happen."

"Maybe it was," I said, finishing my first and last glass of wine.

"Well lets toast," he asked holding up his glass and I grabbed my water.

"What are we toasting to?"

"New friends."

I held my glass out and we clinked to new friends.

PIA KENNEDY

You wouldn't believe the look on my face when I called myself being nice and going to visit Flame to break the tension between us and my visit was denied. By now the guards knew me from visiting Flame at least twice a week, but today they looked at me with some pity in their eyes as they shook their head no. I didn't know what kind of games Flame was playing, but for him to deny my visit or call himself putting me on the "block list" really had soured my entire mood.

I had spent all this time thinking of how I would make things right with him all to get up to the jail to be treated worse than a prisoner. I was about to go slam off, but I remembered that I wasn't even that girl, the girl who made a scene over a man or even the girl who couldn't accept the fact that something was no more. I stomped all the way to my car even pissed at the sun for shining too brightly on me. Once, I finally got in my car I banged my hand against the stirring wheel all the while cursing Flame's name. I know y'all are wondering why I'm so mad but being rejected is the worst for me and Flame knew that based on my past relationships.

I drove off into traffic happy that the jail was only about thirty minutes from my home. I planned to dive straight in my bed while putting my phone on Do Not disturb. I swerved in and out of traffic not giving a damn about the speed limit or stop lights. This was the shit that men did to you, they would have you out driving recklessly not even valuing your own life let alone the life of others.

I started to feel my phone vibrate through my pursed and I fished through it, looking up at the road every few seconds. When I finally found it, I had to mash my damn breaks so hard because I was thirty seconds from ramming into the back of another car.

"Hello!" I answered, frantically.

"Pia, it's me Elle," I heard the voice say and I looked at the screen to see that the number was private.

"Elle, what is up girl and when are you bringing your ass home!" It had been days since Elle had first called me and since then she had been on my mind heavy.

"I'm not coming home Pia, well not anytime soon, but I didn't call to talk about me. How are you?"

I frowned her face up at the phone not believing that Elle would think that she could have a regular conversation when she had been missing for almost two months and had everyone worried to death.

Just when I was about to lay into her ass, I heard the horn beeping from a car that was across from me. I looked over ready to curse whoever out and I noticed that it was the guy, who's car I had hit a couple days ago. He signaled for me to roll down my window as he sat behind a big body Benz smirking. This was the third car that I had seen him with.

I rolled my window down and he started in on me.

"Yo, you so busy yapping on the phone that you are about to cause ANOTHER accident."

"Hello!" Elle said, into the phone and I had forgot that was still there.

"Hold on girl!"

I focused back on Ri and just like the first time I had met him, I noticed how smokin' he was. His big brown eyes paired with his copper colored skin probably drove many ladies wild. He sat there smiling waiting for me to say something, and once I finally snapped out of it, Flame's ugly ass popped in my head making me mad all over again.

"Mind your fucking business!" I snapped back.

"Damn baby, you are spacey just like I like them."

"Spice these nuts nigga!" I said, and then sped off. I didn't have time to go back and forth with him at the light like I didn't have better things to do. Nigga had better get the fuck on.

"PIA PIA! Are you okay?" I heard from the phone.

"Yeah girl. I just had to cuss a nigga out, but how are you though and where are you at?"

"I'm in Ohio, but you cannot tell anyone."

"OHIOOOO!" I yelled. "Girl how did you get there and who the hell would I tell?"

"Really P, you know exactly who you would tell and yeah I just needed a fresh start so here I am."

I pulled up to the Walmart because I needed to get a few things before I went in the house. looking in my rearview mirror, I noticed Ri's smoke gray Benz pulling up behind me. This nigga was asking to be pepper sprayed.

Elle was saying something, and I cut her off. "Girl you need to get your ass home. Calling me from blocked numbers and all of that. Whatever yo' ass did is not that bad! Call me when you are ready for me to book your plane ticket and be safe. Love you," I abruptly hung up the phone before she was even able to respond. I was a little over this Casper the friendly ghost game that she was playing. She needed to face whatever she was running form so that she could move on from it.

"What the hell do you think you are doing?" I asked, as soon as my feet hit the pavement outside of my car.

Ri was just getting out wearing nothing but a tank top and gray jogging pants. My eyes explored his body just until they stopped at his print. This man was standing out here just packing for no reason at all. Once I looked back up he just stood there smirking.

"You like what you see?" he asked.

"Don't get cute! Why are you following me!"

"Shorty last time I checked; this was Walmart, a public place."

"So, out of all of the places you could go, you just happened to be going to Walmart at the same time as me?" I asked.

"Shorty you are wasting my time," he said, with the shake of his head before he walked past me.

I didn't know whether to finish my cursing out or what, but I just stood there standing for a few minutes before finally picked my face up from the ground and went into the store. I grabbed few things and about thirty minutes later when I made it to my car, there was a card attached. I flung it in my purse and made my way home.

SANDY MUGGS

I laid tangled in the sheets after a wild session with my new boy toy, Charles. He was a few years younger than me, but boy could he wear me out. When his gigantic dick was not in my mouth it was in another one of my holes, filling me up completely. The sex between us was amazing, stellar even and he had me ready to make him mine. .permanently.

Like right now, he was in the kitchen making me breakfast after laying it down on me twice. My life was good right now, I had my man and at least one of the Baptist brothers were behind bars where they all belonged. I knew that Kindal would not drop the dime on his brothers, so I had found another avenue to lock all of their black assess up and I would use Spence to do it. Ignitus had been missing from the grid for a while so I wouldn't focus on him. Then there left Shameer and Kiyan.

I didn't want to go after Kiyan because out of all of the brothers he was the most respectable, but I had a feeling that he was down with his brethren's antics as well. He could play that good boy role, but I could see past his little white doctor's coat and his wife, she was a pretty thing, but she had to know if Kiyan was doing anything so, I'm sure I could make her an accessory to his bullshit. I just had to figure out what that bullshit was.

I didn't have cold heard evidence of the things that the Baptists had done, but I do remember a conversation that I heard my father having with one of the brothers. It happened years ago so I can't quite remember who, but what I do remember is hearing them say that the Baptists deserved to burn to burn to death and that the house fire was their way out. From that little statement I knew that they had something to do with the suspicious house fire.

At first, I hadn't planned to do anything with that tad-bit of information, that is up until Shameer rejected me like I was one of those ghetto girls from the block that he was used to dealing with. I didn't take rejection well and after seeing that he wasn't into me like I was him, I came up with a plan to take his ass down, but too bad my father loved them more than he loved me, his own flesh and blood.

"What are you in here daydreaming about?" my boy toy Charles asked. He was holding a tray with breakfast on it and he was naked as the day that he was born.

"You and only you," I said, coyly.

He placed the food down on the bed and I was surprised but it actually looked edible and good.

"This looks delicious," I commented. "I can't wait to dig in," I grabbed the fork and dug I the hash browns.

"Umm, this is almost as good as you," I said, once the ample food was down my throat.

"Almost. I might have to go another round with you to prove you wrong." His sexy ass sounded so good talking his talk. Usually he would have been a little too hood for me, but that is what attracted me to him. I tried to find men who reminded me of Shameer who are nice, clean cut with just a little edge to them and this one here was the closest.

Charles was attractive to say the least and he had the most dazzling eyes that were an interesting mix between hazel and gray. Everything about him just made me want to jump his bones and that is mainly what we did. We fucked and we fucked hard.

Charles plopped down on the bed beside me, his tool looking good enough to eat laying on his leg.

"How is work going?" he stared.

"It's good."

"Everything going well with that case that's been stressing you out lately?"

I looked over to him.

"Stressed? I haven't been stressed," I couldn't believe that he was able to pick up on my nonverbal cues because I had indeed been stressed.

"Come on, we haven't known each other long, but I know you well enough to sense when something isn't right with you."

I debated on whether to let him in on my work life knowing something's that I did weren't by the book, but at the end of the day, I always brought the criminals down.

"Well, its these four brothers that I have been trying to lock up for forever and we just got one so now I'm trying to get the others."

"Well what did they do?" he asked, looking into his phone like he was half interested.

"Well, that the thing. I believe that they have done tons of shit."

"But you don't actually know?"

"Nope, but I'm sure I can dig something up and I will."

There was a brief silence.

"You mean like pin something on them?"

Now he was asking one too many questions and that not what he was here for.

"Why do you have this sudden interest in my job? You want to be a detective or something?"

"Yeah, they are the ones who do the strip searches right?" he asked, moving the plate that was on my lap and inching his hand up my thigh.

"No, that's cops, but you can do whatever you want to do to me baby," I said, with a mischievous grin.

Just when we were about to get into the grove of things, my damn phone rung.

"One second baby," I said ,and then grabbed my phone from the nightstand. It was my partner Spence.

"Talk to me," I answered.

"WHAT!" I screamed, after hearing what he had called me for.

"HOW THE FCK DID THAT SHIT HAPPEN?" I jumped from the bed and straight into the pants that I had had on the previous day.

"You've got to be kidding me Spence. So, the recording just somehow magically disappeared?" To say that I was pissed was an understatement. They were about let anther fucking beast free and hell was going to freeze over if anyone thought that he would stay that way. Damn Kindal Baptist was about to befree.

FLAME BAPTIST

In less than twenty our hours I would be a free man with all charges dropped. I don't know what kind of magic Stephany did, but she had come through and proved herself. I guess she was worth keeping on the team. She was briefing me on keeping my head down and shit once I got out, but I was turning her ass out. I just couldn't wait to get home to my life back. I wasn't locked up for too long, but jail just was for a nigga like me. I would rather die than end up back in this hell hole. Having your freedom taking away was the scariest thing even if it was just for a day.

While thinking about how I would never take my freedom for granted, I couldn't help but think about my girl or lack thereof. Ever since the last argument, that we had had a week ago, I hadn't seen her and when I tried to call her she didn't pick up. I knew she wasn't giving up this easily after a dumb ass argument. If so, she was never with me from the beginning.

"Kindal, hello! Are you listening? You look a little spaced out over there," Stephany snapped at me to get my attention.

"I hear you. Don't do that shit with your fingers to me again."

"What? Snap them?" she asked, puzzled looking down at her fingers.

"Yeah. That shit. And besides everything your saying to me, I've heard me before. This not my first rodeo Pooh."

"Well, I just wanted to reiterate that to you. It seems that Detective Muggs really has something against you and your brothers so she is going to try to pin anything on you that she can. Lay low for a little while," she said, as if she was genuinely interested in my wellbeing.

To be honest Stephany seemed to be the only person who cared besides my brothers. Somehow, she had got my ass out of jail and she was still looking out for a nigga unlike the person who I had been sleeping with before I even came into this bitch.

"Yo, I don't I don't act like it and I'm not always an ass hole, so I wanted to let you know that I have appreciate everything you've done for me thus far. You will be graciously compensated."

"Trust, I know and as good as the money is, that's not what it was about for me. It was for my papa," she pointed, to the sky and I could see the sadness in her eyes. She couldn't even give her father his flowers when he was her because she was facing some demons, but I knew that he was proud of her now.

"And that shit I said when I first met you—" I started.

"Don't worry about it. That's not necessary," she started smiling again while bashfully tucking a lose stand of hair behind her ear.

"So, the next time I see you. You will be a free man. What's the first thing you want to do?"

"Well, I ain't been in here but a lil minute, but I have to get me some Feather N Fin, some smoke and a take along ass bath. I might even use some of the bubble shit that y'all women like."

"Ohhh, bubbles and all! You better show off with your relaxation time," she said, with a laugh causing me to laugh. She thought that I was playing, but that all I wanted to do next to getting some ass, but that was looking like a negative right now unless I hit up one of my baby mamas, which I definitely didn't want to do.

"So, I'm going to go ahead and head back to the office. I have tons of work to catch up on. Hug for the road?" she stretched her arms out and I noticed that she was shaking a little bit as if she was nervous.

I got up from where I was sitting and pulled her into me. I didn't know why she was nervous or scared to share a friendly hug with a nigga like me. Hopefully Muggs would get a life and I would even have to see her anytime soon. Hugging her, I didn't know how little she was compared to me. Pia was 5'5" so Stephany had to be at least five feet eve. My frame swallowed her and as soon as her rich Fawn coated skin, I knew I should've broke the embrace, but I didn't.

I held Stephany for a moment like she was my girl or something when she looked up at me. She looked in my eyes, I guess trying to read me and then she placed her tiny hands on the side of my face. Standing on her tip toes, she pecked my lips and I let the first one slide until she tried it again and I had to stop her. Don't get me wrong I was horny and ready to slide up in anything, but I didn't want to be a dog ass nigga no more. I had to see where me and Pia stood before I jumped in with another bitch literally.

"Okay, I'm going to go. See you around," Stephany said, before picking up her things and dashing for the door. I understood that she was somewhat embarrassed, but I was not about to chase her ass. I had other shit to think about like my freedom and my shorty.

KIYAN BAPTIST

"Five more minutes," I complained, as I hit the snooze button on the alarm clock that was incessantly ringing.

It was going to start ringing like a drum again in another five minutes, but for now that is all that I needed. Five am came too quickly every day and I found myself struggling to get out of bed each morning.

I felt Fancy's small palm gnawing at my shoulder and no matter how many times I hit the snooze button on the clock that stood on my night stand I couldn't snooze her. She would continue to beat my shoulder off until I got up.

"Kiyan, get up! Nobody told you to stay up all night doing god knows what. Go make our baby and me some money."

"You got jokes, huh?" I asked, as I shuffled out of bed, still half sleep. My shift at the hospital started at seven, so I had one hour and a half to get ready and then a twenty-minute drive to get to Chesapeake General. I was glad that I scaled back on my duties at the family barbershop because it was starting to wear me down. Our beard care line was doing well and that would be it for now.

"What were you doing last night anyway? You didn't come to bed till eleven pm?" I looked back to see that Fancy was now sitting u in the bed. Though she was carrying my child and needed her rest, she could never stay asleep when I was getting ready. She complained that I was too loud, and I liked when she was up anyway. Since we had decided to give our marriage another try ,we had really been putting in work getting to know each other all over again so our morning consisted of just that.

I walked up to her and placed a kiss on her lips and then her forehead. One of our past times. There wouldn't be a day that passed that I wouldn't give her a forehead kiss every morning. I knew that I had to love her because, her morning breathe was off the chain and I was still risking my life kissing her.

"I was talking to Miss Candis."

Fancy side eyed me, giving me a skeptical look. She was never the jealous type, but with all of the infidelity that I had caused in our marriage, she made sure she asked more questions these days and she paid attention to everything, hence how she knew that I got in the bed at eleven when she was knocked out snoring by nine.

"You and Miss Candis, sure are chummy. Don't tell me you are into senior citizens now?" she joked.

"You think you are Dave Chapelle this morning, don't you? But nah, you know she be lonely, and she's just taken a liking to me since I met her at the open house," I shrugged. It wasn't that deep to me. The lady didn't have very much family and she was not harming anyone. Over the week that I'd know her we had become close and there was something about her that just made me comfortable.

"Honey, you know I'm just looking but, seriously don't get too attached to this woman. You barely even know her and she does have family and so do you."

I knew exactly what Fancy was getting at. She knew that Family was something that I cherished the most and now she thought that I was getting overly attached. She didn't have to worry about that though aside from her she was carrying the only person that I would ever need. I thought about telling Fancy that I would be meeting Candis for lunch today, but ultimately decided against it. She would just try and talk me out of it and I couldn't bail on the old lady.

Though I dreaded going into work sometimes because the hospital was the nastiest place ever and people came there to die, I really loved my job. Just being able to save a life and even taking someone's pain away really reminded me why I had chosen to become a surgeon in the first place I was I had two more years to go, an addition to a three year years of fellowship and then I would become a surgeon. It turns out that that one year I thought I had left was not accurate. It came down to something about residency hours and paperwork. Residency was proving to be a lot harder and strenuous than medical school which I graduated two years early from when most people took four years or longer finish.

The few six hours of my shift were filled with patching up Boo Boo's and I even had a hernia repair. I checked the time on the clock right above my desk and saw that I was running a few minutes behind on my lunch with Candis. I made my way to the café and got there in about ten minutes, walking. I took in the sweet aroma in the air and I knew that I didn't need a sticky bun, but the little devil on my shoulder was just telling me to go for it.

I grabbed an ice coffee strong and black and yes, I had to get the sticky bun too and looked around form Candis. I didn't see her, so I took a seat and took the time to text my wife.

At the end of the message she agreed to throw dat' ass if I bought her some Sushi home which she craved almost every day since she had been pregnant. I was just about to shoot Candis a text when I looked up at the door and she appeared. She walked up to the table with a smile like she was happy to see me. I got up to pulled her chair out and I noticed a woman walking behind her. I moved out of the walkway so that she could get by but surprisingly she pulled out her seat and sat at our table.

"Oh, baby, this is my niece Kenya, Kenya this is Kiyan the nice young man that I have been telling you about."

I shook her hand unsure of why she was even here and then sat down.

"How has your day gone Candis?" I asked, still feeling kind of weird that we were on a first name basis. Every time I tried to address her as miss, because she was widowed, she corrected me and said that her first name was just fine.

The two of us talked for the next thirty minutes while her niece kind of just sat there. She would steal glances at me and offer a quick word every now and then but for the most part she was basically mute. I didn't know what Candis was up to, but she knew that I was married and we I had met her through my wife. Maybe Faye was right, and I needed to try and distance myself from her a little. I was now understanding that out relationship was a little weird.

I took in one last glance at Kenya before I left to go back to work and I had to admit that she was beautiful, but I wasn't attracted to her at all. She had a butterscotch skin tone and a model build with a natural thing going on with her hair. She gave me a half smile before I left, and I returned it really wondering why the hell she was here.

ELLE LONDON

I couldn't believe that Pia had just hung up on me. I don't know if she called herself telling me off, but to be honest it hurt my feelings. I was so fragile these days that any form of aggression scared and saddened me. I had just caked to make sure that she was okay, but it seemed like she was preoccupied so I will just give her a ring another time.

"What cooking good looking!" Sherry said, when she busted into my room and plopped down on the bed. Here I was minding my business watching Netflix and she had to come to be worrisome like she did every day that she came home from work.

"Hey girl, why you always so damn hyper?" I asked.

Girl because, I have a date tonight and while you're in the house looking sappy on this nice old day, I'm about to have some fun.

"Well, you do that and beside Lex is coming over anyway. He wants me to re-twist his dreads."

"Oh, that not all he wants you to do. Y'all be hanging out like crazy. I know you feeling that fine ass nigga," she was practically fanning herself, but what's she didn't know is what she was saying was the furthest from the truth. Yeah, Lex is attractive and when I first saw him a couple of nasty thoughts crossed my mind, but after that day those premature feelings had vanished for no particular reason at all. I wasn't about to jump into something else so soon anyway so my cousin could cross that off her list.

"Girl, we are not feeling each other, just cool."

"Yeah whatever. I know you not over your old flame yet and that's why you won't let Lex's jump your bones."

I had told her little about Smoke and now she couldn't stop bringing is ass up. It was even to the point where she wanted me to pull up his social media so that she could see him. Honey was pressed, no space bar.

"That is funny because he has a brother named Flame. He's what one would call a livewire."

"Oh, he's a live wire, I bet he could put something on my ass if he looks anything like his brother."

"Slow your role slim. He's with my friend. All of the Baptist brothers are taken actually except Smoke now," I said, sadly.

I could feel the tear about to come and I turned away from Sherry. My stupid heart. Why was I so attached to this man that I knew I couldn't be with? In the short time that Smoke and I had known each other he had made me feel like the only girl in the world. I remember the first time I met him like it was yesterday. He chased me down after I kept giving him someone else's meal. If I wasn't smitten then, I definitely was after our first date.

I mourned at the death of our relationship and the secrets that I was keeping from him. I never knew that I had the ability to become this person that was lying and sneaking around like my parents had raised me with no moral at all. No matter how much I tried to move past everything I still felt stuck.

"Girl, you better not be over there crying. I done seen you cry every day that you been here. Your date will be here soon so you better wipe then snot boogers from your face."

I turned over to face her with a slight smile. She had a way of lifting me when I was down.

"It is not a date," I said, while laughing.

"Well, girl go blow your nose and help me get ready for mine then."

She gave me one last smile and a squeeze on my thigh before she sprinted to her room.

Two hours later and a Fenty beat by me, my cousin was ready for her date. She was really into this dude because she made sure to go all out for this date and even though I felt little congested and my back was killing me, I still did her makeup which took me an hour to do.

"Okay, girl. I will see you a little later, call me if you need anything," she said, pulling down the red halter dress that she was wearing.

"Okay mom doesn't do anything that I wouldn't do," I said, with a smile.

"Uhh huh Chica and the same goes for you," she grabbed her keys and she was out of the door to her date.

I went and hopped in the shower before Lex texted me saying that he was on his way asking did I want anything to eat. I told him whatever he got was fine, but I was now feeling a little awkward after my talk with Sherry. I didn't want to lead Lex on, but I was definitely not into him. We had spent some time together, but it was on always on some chill buddy-buddy type stuff. I just figured we were both new to town and didn't know anyone.

After my shower, I applied some mango shea butter to my body and noticed that my shape was changing. With me not being really active lately and trying to shield myself from society, I stayed in stuffed my face. One thing that didn't changed during my depressive stated was my eating habits, if anything it increased.

Slipping into one of my old college oversized sweatshirts and a basic pair of leggings, I heard my phone chime signaling that Lex as at the door.

—"Yo, yo," he said, as soon as I opened the door. That was hat he said every time he greeted me. It had only been a little over a week and he had been over at least four times and in that times, I learned a little about him. He had come to Ohio for a business opportunity with his uncle and get this, he had grown up in Virginia. It was d a small world that though I hadn't grown up in Virginia, but most of my adulthood was there and I had never crossed paths or heard of Lex before.

Lex had brought us some burgers, fries and shakes and by the time I finished it all, I was stuffed and not in the mood to twist his Dreads that damn near came to his ass. I was ready to lay it down, but I wouldn't do him like that.

"Come on big head, let's get to it," I said, sitting on the couch and opening my legs for him to sit in between them. I turned on some old school Keyshia Cole when she was Falling out and just wanted it to be over and I was done his hair in no time. He was knocked out in between my legs and I had managed to twist his hair in one hour and thirty minutes.

I tapped his shoulder lightly and he jumped up causing me too to laugh.

"What are you laughing at?" he asked, getting up and stretching.

"You, jumping like your crazy. You weren't even sleep that long."

"Man, you in my head felt good as hell and put me to sleep instantly. Your hands must be magical or something."

"Maybe," I said. moving my hands like I was playing the piano.

"Well, sir. I Hate to kick you out, but I'm am dead tired. You don't have to go home, but... well you know the rest," I said, jokingly.

"Dammmnnn, it's like that," he stroked his chin while giving me this look. I couldn't read it, but it made me feel a little nervous.

Lex then reached into his pockets and pulled out a knot. He flicked three crispy one-hundred-dollar bills away and handed them to me.

"What! Stop playing. You know I would not take your money for that," I lied. The truth is I was broke as hell and needed anything that he would give, but I didn't want to seem like some kind of bum .

"Aite. I will leave this. You don't have to take it, but I know your greedy as cousin will," we both laughed. I was going to scoop that up a soon as he left.

"Aye watch your mouth," I said, throwing air punches.

He then walked past me, his jeans riding his butt so that I could see his Polo boxers. Before he could get to the door he turned around and suddenly kissed me HARD. I couldn't even pull back because his tongue seemed to be stuck in my throat.

"Wa waaa," I tried to say while waving my hands in the air before he finally removed his oversized lips from around mine.

"What was that?" I asked trying to catch my damn breath. "Lex, I'm not feeling you like that and I think that you should go."

"Damn, my bad I thought that we were on the same page."

"Not at all. You're on page eight-six and I'm on page one. Please go," I pointed to the door and he apologized again before leaving.

After locking the door, I had to laugh because this negro and really just tried to swallow my damn face. It wasn't sexy at all and now I for sure knew that I was definitely not into him. That was one nasty wet nasty ass kiss!

SCAR BANKS

⚮

The incessant tapping of my fingers against the brown wooden table in addition to the slowly ticking clock that sat above my head was just about to drive me insane. Once again I was waiting in the ice-cold visiting room for my brother to come out. It had been thirty minutes already and my patience was running thin and when that happened shit got hectic.

Staring own at the table I couldn't help but think of the countless people who had sat at this table in my exact same spot. Numerous words and names word scattered throughout the wood like it was a high school desk or something. Seeing Tay Tay loves Leah made me smile a little. Tay Tay loved that girl so much that he waited to come to a jail visit to scribble the shit on a table.

That only occupied my time for a few seconds as I looked up at the clock for the twentieth time wondering why they liked to fuck with my time here.

"Yo, fuck is up with this visit," I turned back and looked at the CO who was just idly standing not doing a damn thing.

"What do you mean?" he asked, with a hint of bout its bout it in his voice.

I got up so he could feel just exactly what I meant.

"What I mean is, I been in this bitch for damn near an hour waiting to see my brother," I growled at him. "Fuck type time all on in this bitch B?"

Now his ass was shaking and that hype that he had in voice before had magically disappeared.

"I will go see what is taking them so long to bring them down," he scurried his fat ass away and in less than five minutes Jacob came limping out.

My eyes widened in disbelief when he finally got to the table and I looked him in his face. Dark rings were around his eyes, his lip was busted and from the look on his face I could tell that he was in pain. I clasped my hands together and said a silent prayer so that whoever was up in the sky could control the anger that I was feeling right now.

"What happened to you Jacob?" I asked, trying to contain the beast that was about to erupt from me.

"Nothing, a little fight that's all," he tried his best to sugarcoat the shit which got me even more upset.

"Tell, me the Truth Co. Either way shit gone get handled."

He tried his best to see out of his broken glass, but they ultimately fell into his lap. He was nervous, but more than that he was scared.

"Co, let me help you," I pleaded with him.

"No, I don't need your help. Just do what you said you were going to. That is the only way."

I rubbed my hands over my face out of frustration. My plan to get my brother out was coming along, but it wasn't coming along fast enough. It was coming up on a year that he had been in this bitch and the first half, I was locked up so he had some bullshit ass court appointed lawyer who didn't know his face from his ass hole and now here we are.

"Jacob you have to hold on in here and be strong. I'm moving trust me, but in the meantime, you have to be strong and defend yourself and most of all you have to tell your big brother the truth."

He covered his face and I could tell that he didn't want me to see him cry. Jacob was always this way. Growing up, he was pretty much a good kid who made straight as and played field hockey. The street shit that I was into didn't interest him and he stayed on the straight and narrow up until the shit he got into his junior year.

"Now, tell me what happened. What really happened?"

"People just fuck with me in here. Every day it is something new, but last night when I was coming out of the shower, I was attacked by a gang of them. I didn't see who they were though."

I knew his ass was straight up lying. Niggas beating your ass and you didn't get one look at any of them. He just didn't want to tell me because he knew that I would do anything for him and that included risking my own freedom.

"It's this one guy named Flame that tries to look out for me, but he is about to be released," Jacob added.

"Don't worry about it. You don't have to worry about shit! I got some *OHs* who gone watch you while you are in here. All I have to do is make that call. You have to just keep your head up boy!"

Co nodded and for the rest of the visit we sat silently. It was staring me up inside that I couldn't do more for my brother but, he would be home soon. I just had a couple more moves to make and he would never have to see the inside of this place ever again.

PIA KENNEDY

*S*oon *as I jumped into my ride those memories start to Playaway. A song comes on, on the radio and there you are baby once again. It's just another sad love song rocking my brain like crazy, guess I'm all torn up. Be it fast or slow it doesn't let go of SHAKE me ouuh and it's all because of yoouuu!*

Toni Braxton's *Another Sad love song* played on repeat as I was finally feeling the downside of the possible end of my relationship with Flame. At first, I was a little mad and probably doing too much, but I didn't think that we would end. We argued and just needed some space, but for him to refuse my visit told me that he was officially done with me.

The anger and irrationality had dissipated and now the hurt and the lugubrious was starting to sink in. No way we were over so soon when we had made so many plans. No way, I wasn't worth him fighting for me and me fighting for him. It was crazy how just a day ago, I was so quick to say fuck him and now here I was alone not having to wear that façade, empty.

I laid in bed wrapped around my body pillow sobbing into my arm while Toni sung the soundtrack to my relationship. And to make things even more awkward everything reminded me of this man from the song that was playing, to his scent that I could never wash out of my pillows and even his t-shirt that I was sleeping in right now. This feeling though, I knew that I was sad and mostly defeated, but this feeling was one that I had never experienced in any relationship.

This feeling overwhelmed me and took the presence of anything that was good. Nothing was good for me and I wished that I could just pick up the phone to call Flame and express myself and curse him out, but I couldn't. I didn't even know anything regarding his case or anything and I had taken a few days off from work, so I hadn't seen his brother to even ask.

Flame was literally consuming my thoughts and it damn near made it impossible for me to do or think of anything constructive. I had laid in the same spot all damn day, the same song played and the same ache pierced m heart. Being in Love was a mutherfucka and this was the first time that I even used the L word so I knew that after this, I would be through with relationships. It would be back to the pompous Pia who enjoyed dick and putting men on do not disturb shortly after.

I rolled over wiping my tear stained face and felt something stickling my side. When I looked under the duvet cover, it was a card. I read it and it was Ri's card for his detailing shop. I wondered how it got tangled in my sheets and why he had even given it to me in the first place. The last thing on my mind was getting my damn car cleaned, I needed m damn life cleaned. Where the hell was Iyanla? Maybe Tomorrow would be better.

FLAME BAPTIST

I busted up out of them gates screaming fuck the law vowing to never return. Even the air felt different once you crossed the line that separated you from being a normal human being from a convict. I don't care if I had to murk Muggs ass, that bitch would never catch me slipping ever again.

I heard the sound of a horn honking and looked over to see a nice ass Lexus Jeep. Shit was a sight for sore eyes, and I couldn't wait to get behind the wheel of one of my babies. I wouldn't call myself a car fanatic, but I owned three luxury cars and traded them shits in yearly on a whim.

I heard the horn honk again and I tried to narrow my eyes to see who it was, but the tints were too dark.

"Come on silly," I heard the familiar voice and I was surprised to see Stephany peek her head out of the window.

"Yo what are you doing here?" I asked, caught off guard. She was sitting behind her wheel smiling like she had just won the lottery.

"Well, I know now that your brother was supposed to be here, but I told him I would scoop you instead. I was already up here anyway with another client."

I side eyed her for a moment. Stephany seemed like a cool girl, but it was clear that she was already catching feelings. I debated whether or not I should leave with her and then just said fuck it. I was ready to get far away for this shit hole. I hopped in her whip and changed the girly shit that she was playing. I hooked my phone up that I got out of the brown paper bag that ad all my belongings from when I first got locked up. I hooked it up to her radio and blasted that *Lil Durk x David Ruffin.*

You ever woke up out your sleep like is you gon' die in the trenches?
You ever thought it'd be your dawg when they described the witness?
I wrote a letter to authorities when they threw out the tenants
To claim that shit that bro'nem claim, you know that shit a privilege
For Pat I'll throw them tears, I remember the night they took him
I treat them hoes with a lil' respect cause that could be my sister
They had gave police them guns, when they pulled up, they booked 'em
We catch a opp, he get baptized like I was never Muslim
Like wipe yo' nose, I love you bro, stop fucking with Ashton Kutcher

I banged that shit a hunnid times before I finally made it to my destination. I caught Stephany off beat bobbing her head a few times and it made me chuckle. Yeah, she was Italian and black, but to me she was whit. She looked white and talked white so her ass was white to me.

I got out of the car and nodded to her and thanked her for the ride and she smiled before stopping me.

"Oh, and I know that you are not driving so I can pick you up when you are done," she said, hopefully.

"Nah, I'm good baby, one of my brothers got me."

"Oh, if they are at work you don't have to bother them. Just text me," she was damn near begging now and it was not becoming of her.

"Shorty, fix your face. You want to be my chauffeur that damn badly?" I stroked my chin while she only looked on.

My own bitch didn't know that I was out and probably didn't care to see so why would I turn down Stephany. She could be my driver for the day.

"Aite, come back and get me in an hour. Don't be taking all day either," I'm sure if I asked her ass to sit outside and wait for me, she would.

"Okay," she said, with a perky smile. I shook my head and walked off. This bitch had it bad.

"FIRST OF ALL, FUCK YA BITCH AND THE CLIQUE YOU CLAIM!" I announced my presence walking into the Smokin' Kutz.

It was Friday and the shop was packed as hell. The weather was still pretty nice out so that was an added plus for the shop. Kids was running around; each chair was filled and as usual I had interrupted some deep ass conversation piece or something.

"My boy!" Iggy was the first to approach me and gave me a big ass bear hug. This man really thought he was my daddy. He had to get his hug in first.

"Oh, nigga so you back from that fancy ass island with Beau. I thought you was about to become a citizen or something," I joked.

"Man, your shit talking ass starting up already. Somebody come get him."

All the patrons were dapping me up welcoming me home and I made sure to hug each of my brothers. You know hugs were our thing. It connected us and we never ended the day without giving one another at least one hug.

"They done let Flamin Flame out. Hide your kids hide your wives," Smoke said, causing the shop to erupt in laugher.

I could only shrug because the he was right. The beast was back.

I couldn't hold it in any longer. "Yo, P here?" I looked at each of my brothers.

"Nah, she been out for a few days bruh bruh," Smoke replied.

"Oh, aite," I tried playing it off, but my brothers knew me too well.

"Trouble in paradise already?" Kiyan asked.

"Mann, let fools. I haven't seen the her in 'bout three weeks and she supposed to be my girl Fuck her!" I went a little overboard with the time.

"Aye watch yo mouth boy!" Iggy corrected me, but shit that's how she was acting.

"But anyway, on to greener pastures," I shrugged nonchalantly.

"And your new boo, I mean lawyer let us know that she was picking you up. Don't tell me you fucked that white girl." Smoke was cracking up.

"Man nah, but she definitely on the kid. This dick will probably have her traumatized and delusional I will pass on the headache," I waved my hand as if I was waving her off.

"But what's new with y'all niggas. I feel like it's been forever, and I know y'all couldn't say much on them people's phones," I referred to the jail phones.

"Pretty boy, what happening?" I turned to my brother Kiyan.

"Everything is cool on my end. Faye and me good and we just waiting for lil' baby to arrive. We decided to wait until the birth to find out what the sex is."

"You know I'm going to spoil the hell out of whatever it is. You know Flame love the kids," I impersonated Martin.

"Oh, and I wanted to let y'all in on something to. I saw Hector the other day at his little sot and he kind of slipped up and said that he saw Sandy creeping out of the hospital right around the time when Pops passed. It just seemed crazy to me that no one knew that she was even there."

"Word, so you think she may have had something to do with Pop's death?" I asked trying to piece together what he was saying.

"If the shoe fits," Kiyan shrugged.

We all kind of stood there in deep thought. We all knew that Muggs was shady, but never did we think that she would sink that low.

"Man, I thought that that girl would be gotten some help by now," Iggy shook his head. Hopefully she didn't do that shit.

We all nodded knowing even if she did, we would never be able to prove it.

I noticed that Smoke was looking a little odd.

"Smoke, you linked up with runaway love yet?" I couldn't help but laugh at his situation. The girl had left him, and he was shown up at her people's house trying to track her down. He was pathetic.

"Man, I'm not even on that," was all he replied. In his feelings was a bad place to be fucking with my joking ass and I could tell that there was something that he wasn't saying. I was free, happy and was ready to joke all their asses under the table.

"And I guess I don't have to ask about you father time. But Beau good though?" I asked, being concerned. I knew that Beau was battling stomach cancer and my brother was happy with her, so I was genuinely concerned.

"Yeah, she is doing great actually. She has her good and her bad days but being able to lay on the beach everyday soaking under the sun was really healing for her. After almost a month she still dint want to leave, but my pockets were saying otherwise."

Father time paused for a moment and looked at each of us before he resumed talking. Even in a packed ass shop we had tuned everyone out and talked amongst each other. Iggy and Smoke never stopped cutting through and as focused as we were on this conversation, they were more focused on their craft.

"So, I been thinking. I don't know whether I'm ready to talk to Beau about dancing. I know I can't go forever keeping this from her, I just don't how she would take the shit."

"Glad my wife dances too," Kiyan said, with a sigh of relief.

It was true, Kiyan had trained Faye's ass and now she was as deadly as him and she had her daddy on her side being district attorney. If there was any movement in the streets, she knew so that meant we knew.

Our alternate lifestyle is what we referred to as "dancing." When we were in the company of others. It was another source of income, a street sweep and most of all killing with a cause.

Up until now I hadn't even thought about relaying my entire past to Pia. I had told her about the Baptists, but that wasn't nearly everything. As far as she knew, I was just a nigga who owned a barbershop, gave good dick and a had thug mentality. She didn't know that the two-step was my specialty.

"I say, fake it till you make it. Leave that shit alone and don't tell her anything," I offered.

"Man, you don't think any of our girls gone start to get suspicious by the way we move. We can't go forever hiding it," Smoke chimed in.

"Nigga, ain't no we. Yo' as is single as a pringle. You don't have to worry about telling anybody anything and neither do I. Dot nobody belong to us," I reminded him. His ex-girl was probably in Guatemala by now.

"Okay, so hypothetically speaking, if you were still with Pia and Smoke, if you were still with Elle. Y'all wouldn't say anything ever?" Kiyan asked.

I didn't even know why he was mentioning me and that girl's name in the same sentence. Fuck the hypotheticals.

"I would tell her eventually and it would be her decision to stay or go." Smoke shrugged.

"So, you would risk your freedom, all because you in strong like with her?" I asked, not getting where his allegiance to Elle came from. Clearly, she had some sneakiness to her the way she just up and left.

"Bottom lined, Flame whether you agree or not. You can't expect to build some shit with a person having so many lies and secrets going on. Eventually, that shit get tiring having to lie about what you were doing or who you are with. If she solid, she gone be down for you regardless." Father time offered and I listened. He was usually the one who could talk some sense into me, but pia had definitely proved that she couldn't be trusted with anymore of my secrets.

"Now, how you should tell is a whole other story," Smoke looked over at Iggy.

"No doubt, but I'ma figure this shit out."

Tired of waiting I went over to Iggy's chair. "Yo, get up," I said to the person who was about to be serviced. Dude, who didn't know got up and I sat down in the chair.

"Iggy don't fuck my shit up," I barked, while the man just stood there waiting. For what I didn't know.

"Father time tell your customer to carry his happy ass and have a seat. He's next."

Iggy tried to hide his laughter and told the man that his hair cut would be next, and it would be on the house.

"Man, jail isn't do you no good. Still rude and egregious," he commented

"You love me though. I got to get up out of here thou. A nigga needs a shower, blunt and y'all. know the rest."

About thirty minutes later Iggy had hooked me up and I said my goodbyes to my brothers because I had to get cleaned up so that I could go and see my babies. Ai missed them like crazy even though neither one of their moms answered the phone when I was locked up. As if I wanted to talk to their stinking asses. They were going to get a mouthful.

"Aye boy! Make sure you lay low. And BE CARFUL!" Iggy said as I was walking at the door and I nodded assuring him that I knew what time it was.

When I got outside, Stephany was waiting for me. I got in the car brushing my hair and she looked me up and down with a hungry look in her eyes. It was something about a nigga and a fresh cut that made women want to shoot yo' your mama crib over you. I wasn't on that type of time though. Shorty was giving off mad clingy vibes and I didn't like Pussy that came with expectations. Her ass still was going to drive me around though.

PIA KENNEDY

I stepped out of my car and looked around skeptically before spotting the voice that I was looking for. What made me come here, I didn't know, but it was on my way home from the nail shop, so I just stopped by. After a day of moping and feeling sorry for myself, I had managed to get up, clean my house and run some errands. After relaxing at the nail spa, I was feeling a little better, but I wasn't at one hundred percent yet.

"You don't have to look so scared, we don't bite around these parts," I heard a voice say to me and when I turned around it was some dude that I didn't know. He was eying me up and down like he wanted to eat me through my socks with these blue overalls on. It was very intimidating because he didn't even try to hide it.

"Aye, Fred her ass ain't scary by no means. Trust me I've felt her before."

Now that voice I knew.

"So, you decided to finally come and get that dirty ass car cleaned miss lady?" Ri asked and by the smile that was plastered on his face, I didn't know if he had been waiting for my arrival or if he always looked this stupid.

"I'm here," I said, unenthusiastically. "So, don't be trying to charge me five hundred dollars for a wash and cleaning." I knew how these men would try to get over on gullible females when it came to their cars.

"Now, why would I do that? Your money is no good here love."

Some man came up and got my keys and then drove my car around back, letting me now that it would be about thirty minutes.

"BIIITTTCH INCHESSS!" I heard a loud voice yell from behind me and when I turned around, I was met with this lady with big hair, big tits and an even bigger personality.

"Sis! The bundles," she commented and now I knew that she was referring to my twenty-eight-inch Brazilian deep wave that I had in my hair.

"Ohhh, thank you," I chuckled at her boldness. Baby was sporting lime green lipstick and a one piece even though she looked a little hefty. She wore it well though.

"Eva, carry yo' talking ass. Don't run my new friend off," he said to her. By now I could tell that Eva may have used to be an Evan and that was fine with me.

"Khiri, please. This girl is too pretty for your kind."

"Damnnnn that hurt my soul," he clutched his heard acting like he was hurt.

I just sat there and enjoyed the show while they went back and forth with jokes cracking me up.

FLAME BAPTIST

We pulled up to my crib and I got out. I was gone made her ass wait in the car, but she had copped some smoke and backwoods for me so the least I could let her do was sit on my couch.

"Aye, I will be back. I'm about to shower and dressed and shit. Don't touch nothing!" I warned Stephany.

She smiled that ditzy ass smile and nodded her head. I was noticing that she was a lot different outside of her lawyer duties. Then, she was very direct and thorough and now she was like a love struct puppy that was waiting to get blown down by the fireman. Speaking of, I knew that I had a lot of hits to make so my work would continue soon.

I walked into my room and just being in my own space and in the comfort of my own home bought me solace. My bedroom, always tidy had a coat of dust that had formed along the dressers and the pillows on my bed had fallen a little from not being fluffed over the months. I handled those two situations and then did exactly what I said I wanted to for when I got out. I ran a bath and lighted a big fat joint.

Y'all, don't come for a nigga either for taking a bath, but after being in jail the shit is needed. I'm still a thug at heart willing to show you better than I could tell you. After about ten minutes of just sitting there, I couldn't get with the shit, so I stood my big self-up and finished off with a shower. I looked in the closet for something to wear and a nigga didn't even have to go to the mall. Almost everything hanging still had tags, so I decided to go with my signature look, a designer pair of jeans, two chain, no shirt and the classic Concord Jordans .

Like a nigga, it didn't take me long to get dressed and I rolled me another L. I was feeling right and just happy to be home, so I caught myself just looking in the mirror smiling, high as a mutherfucker. Looking at my Patek, I saw that I had had the girl waiting for me for an hour and a half, so I decided to get on move on. I half-way expected her ass to be gone, but when I grabbed my Versus Versace Backpack and went down the stair, she was waiting patiently typing away on her phone. She was probably telling her lil' girlfriends that she had met a real one.

As if he could since my presence she looked up and instantly a smile came across her face. I could tell that she was really liking the kid outside of my jail threads.

"You ready?" I asked her.

"Yeah, we can go wherever, but I just have to make one stop first. Is that cool?"

"Fosho, just don't take all day, I have to go see my kids," I missed my babies more than anything when I was locked up behind that wall.

"Perf!" she said, and then she hopped up from the couch and walked to the door. All the while she hawked my ass. I couldn't help but shake my head and laugh. I searched my liquor cabinet and poured myself so Henn dog, just for a slight buzz. I know that I couldn't go around my girls drunk so I would tread lightly.

"Can I have some?" Stephany asked as soon as I sat my ass on her leather buttery seats.

I looked at her trying to see if she was serious or not and she was.

"You drink Henny girl? This is a man's drink."

"I really don't drink at all."

"Oh, yea, I forgot. The harder shit is your choice," I said, and took another sip of the brown that was in my cup.

"I will just take a sip," she said, before I finally passed her the red plastic cup.

She tried to be a big girl and instead of the sip that she promised, she took a gulp and ended up in a fit of coughs. I couldn't help but laugh.

"Look at you trying to be big dawg," I continued to chuckle and grabbed my cup out of her hand.

"Now come on baby, lets blow this money," I increased the volume of the music and laid back until we got to her destination. No too long after, we pulled up to a shop, it looked like it could have been a detailing shop.

"Your car wash couldn't wait?" I asked.

"It actually couldn't. this shop is really popular, and I made my appointment a month ago. That's is how busy they are."

I looked at the numerous people standing around and it looked like a block party or some shit. I had never heard of this establishment, but it seemed to be doing very well.

I rolled up another spliff in the car while she waited to be serviced. I tucked my nine too, because there were plenty niggas out here for me not to be scrapped. Some dude finally came to get Stephany's car and he was all in her grill. I didn't give the slightest fuck, hopefully he could take her off my hands. We got out to walk to the lounge/waiting area because I was not about to kick it and parlay with a bunch of niggas that I didn't know, when I was spotted.

"Aye yo Flizzy Flame." The only person who called me that was this dumb fuck named Sherman, he was a young boy. I looked around to see hm approaching me and I realized that just off the strength of who I am. Everywhere I went, there would be pp who knew me. I was legendary in the hood.

"What's up Sherm Sherm?" I dapped him up once he reached me.

"Welcome back my boy!" he smiled.

"Thanks man."

"Welll, you are looking good, like money," he joked.

"Man, get out of here. I'm regular," I joked back.

"We glad you home man, the hood been missing you. You here to meet your girl?"

My eyebrows crinkled.

"Yeah, she over there man," he pointed.

I looked over, and there was Pia. She hadn't been answering my calls, but she had the time to be posted up at a weak ass car wash and to top it off she was laughing with her hand posted on a nigga chest. I felt myself about to blow up and the type of person I was, I showed my ass first and asked questions later. Sherman was still running his trap when I walked off.

The nigga parted fast than a skeezers legs when I walked through, because they may have not known me, but they definitely knew of me. They even nodded as a sign of respect.

I walked over to where Pia and whoever were standing, and I didn't have to say anything to her. She felt my presence. She turned around and the shock was written all over her face.

"Kindal," she called out. She looked like she wanted to smile, but she also knew that she was in a fucked-up position.

"Introduce me to your friend P," I told her, this was the calm before the storm.

Pia looked into my eyes and she already knew what type of party this was about to be.

"Flame," she shook her head no. " I'm just here getting my car washed, that's all," she pleaded with me with her eyes.

"Fuck this poor ass car wash Let's GO!" I said, with a sharp tone and she immediately bobbed her head up and down, knowing she didn't want to be further embarrassed.

"P, you good," the dude asked her and then he had a nerve to grab her by the hand.

Casanova was definitely about to meet his match.

"Yeah, she good playboy, she is always good. So, before shit gets unruly, I suggest you get back to washing these fucking cars."

Just then, I heard a voice from behind me.

"Babe, is everything okay?" Stephany had the nerve to come up behind me rubbing my back.

If Pia had any remorse before, it was gone now.

"Babe?" Pia questioned with a smile. This wasn't a happy smile though.

"This you?" she asked. Now she was just being funny.

I inched away from Stephany. "We not about to discuss this out here," I looked at Pia.

"Oh, we are!" Pia said, nodding her head up and down and that weak ass smile never left her face. "So, who is she?"

"I'm Stephany, nice to meet you."

"My lawyer," I cut in before she could say anything else. This bitch was about to get smacked the shit out of. She clearly was on some funny shit the way she looked at Pia with Envy in her eyes.

"Let's go Pia," I said, again and gently grabbed her arm.

"Nah. I'm not going anywhere. Continue enjoying your day with you lawyer," she used air quoted and grabbed her arm causing me to let out a tiring sigh.

"Gladly, we've been together all day anyway. Flame lets go BACK to your house," she asked, me putting emphasis on back and Pia's eyes widened like saucers.

I was trying to spare this bitch because she had just got me out, but now she was taking it to far.

"Carry yo' dick riding ass yo'. You got me fucked up if you think you about to stand here and come for my girl. Stick to the mutherfucking role that I pay you for!" I snapped, finally tie of the fucking shenanigans. People were just standing around watching this shit go down and I didn't give a fuck.

Stephany looked like she was about to ball her fucking eyes out .

"Fuck out of here Junkie," I said, putting the final nail in Stephany's coffin. The bitch could relapse for all I care, but she had really showed her ass tonight like there was ever anything between us.

Stephany took off running and Pia got satisfaction out of that. She even stuck her tongue out and waved goodbye to her.

"You, let's go!" I said, for the final time and walked off. Pia knew to follow me and just as I suspected she was right on my heels.

PIA KENNEDY

Flame drove his friend's car to my home, and I drove mine. There was no way his insane ass was riding with me. I thought that he was going to go to his house to cool off, but when I parked in my driveway, he was right behind me. He was definitely going to be on some bullshit tonight and so was I. I didn't know who that raggedy butch was or why she was at his damn house, but I was going to find out. I dint even know that he was out of jail so aside from that I felt like I was being ambushed.

I stormed into the house closing the front door right in his face. I didn't even care that he had just embarrassed the hell out of me in front of all the people, but I was more furious about the little arm candy that he was sporting.

"Aye P, remember I'm home now, so you can stop trying me with all of that slick shit," he said, walking into the house.

By now, I had downed two shots in the kitchen and I was waiting for him so we could get some things straight.

He walked into the kitchen without saying a word, only staring like he was stupid.

"Okay, so first question. Why didn't I know that you were home?

TESHERA C.

Matter fact when did you even get out?" I flung my hands in the air hoping that it would emphasize my point.

He shook his head, "I just came home today and how was I supposed to tell you when you was not answering my calls and hadn't even been to see me? That shit was foul as hell!"

"Well, I don't recall missing any calls, but when I came to see your ass you took me off your visit list."

Flame's eyes busked as if what I was saying was from far away land.

"Don't look like that nigga, speak!" I snapped.

He laughed how he always did when he was trying to control his anger.

"I didn't refuse no fucking visit, so I don't know where you got that from."

"Well If you didn't, who did? When I got up there, they turned me around."

He looked to be in deep thought and then his head dropped as if whatever he was searching for came to him.

"This shit crazy. I didn't your visit, but I think I know who did."

"Ohhhokayy," I said waiting for him to spit it out.

"It had to have been Stephany, my lawyer."

"Ohhhhhh, which brings me to my second question. WHAT THE HELL WAS BECKY WITH THE GOOD HAIR DOING AT YOU HOUSE? WHAT WAS SHE DOING WITH YOU PERIOD?"

"Man, you want to play twenty-one questions with me like I didn't have to practically just drag your from your little car washing friend."

"So, this is what we're going to do? Just turn all of this on me because your shit stinks? I was doing exactly what I was supposed to be doing at a car wash, GETTING MY CAR WASHED DUMB DUMB! I don't know what you think you saw, but maybe it was your guilty conscious kicking in. My boyfriend gets out of jail and I'm the last to know. You know my number and address so don't even act like you was even checking for me!" I was heated and on a roll.

"Okay, I'm going to let you get your shit off. Keep it up," he tossed idle threats.

"So, answer my question. What was Becky doing at your house!"

"I told you before, she is my lawyer, the one I told you about. She scooped a nigga from the yard because my girl couldn't," he made sure to throw that part in as if he had even given me a choice to pick him up.

"She asked me if she could drive me around for the day and that was that," he said nonchalantly as if any of what he was saying was right on his part.

"Okay, so get to the point where y'all went to your house."

He let out a sigh, "I took a shower and she waited for me. ain't much to tell and then we rolled out."

"This is unbelievable," I said, while trying not to cry and looking up at the ceiling.

"Did you have sex with her?" I asked lowly.

"Pia come on," his tone was now softer and he rushed over to me. "I ain't touch that girl let alone fuck her."

"And how and I supposed to believe that the way she was acting tonight?"

"And I straightened her right? Nothing happened bae."

"Don't call me that," I said backing away from him. I didn't trust a thing that he was saying, and I still couldn't get over me not even knowing that he was a free man.

"P, I'm going to keep it a humid with you because I don't have shit to hide. I could've fucked her if I wanted to, but I didn't take it there with her. She was throwing me little vibes all day, but I wasn't on that type of time. She did try to kiss me, but I cut that off too, because of you. Even if we were on bad terms, I couldn't do you like that."

Silence floated in the air between us and I didn't know if I was on the verge of tears or wanted to accept the bullshit that he was feeding me.

"Get out Flame," I said, lowly.

"What?" he asked, caught off guard.

"I said get out!" This time he heard me much more clearly.

"Pia, you know I'm not leaving this fucking house. I didn't fuck that girl, nor am I into her and I will never be."

"I don't believe you; I mean look at the way I had to find out. If the script was flipped an I was riding around with random guy, letting you know that they wanted to fuck me and all that. I don't think that you would be as calm as I am now."

"Bae, I will fire the bitch. I will never talk to her again," he was pleading with me now and that macho man act that he carried on was not there anymore.

I looked at him with my head tilted not really knowing what to say. More than anything I was embarrassed.

"Flame, I hear all that you are saying, but I would still like for you to leave. "

"I can do that, because I fucked up, but Pia we are going to be together forever. Believe that," he pecked my lips and then he left.

SMOKE BAPTIST

"So, you have five now? Y'all haven't been playing any games," I said, to the customer that was in my chair. Him and his girl was on baby number five to my zero.

"Yeah, man she can't keep her hands off me, but we are done at this one."

"Man, you said that when y'all had Blix. I hear you though," I laughed.

"What about you though? You want kids?" he asked me, and I really had to think about that question.

Sometimes I thought that I was just way too fucked up from my childhood to raise a kid. I would hate to turn into anything relatively close to the Baptist and fuck a kid up. For me, it wouldn't be no kids today tomorrow or the day after that. I was focused on my money and that's about it

"Man, I'm good on that for now, don't be trying to put nothing on me bruh. I'm clean," I joked.

"And you and the shorty I saw you with good?" Kassidy had to have been talking about Elle. We had bumped into him a while back.

"Man, I don't even really know what to say about that. She is doing her and I'm doing me."

TESHERA C.

"Oh word. Don't sweat that shit though. You know how many times me and Bliss was doing us?" he air quoted the doing us part.

"Them make up to break up's make you really see what is important and if that person is really down for you. I can tell that you like her from the way your mood changed when I asked you about her. Play that shit how it goes, anything worth having is worth fighting for. Hell! My girl accepted me back after I faked my own death," he joked and shook his head.

I thought about what he said and wondered if Elle showed back in my life today could I accept the fact that she just up and left me. I would definitely have to choke her as up first, but I feel like things would never be the same between us. And the way that little message that her sister gave me when I was at their house let me know that she had some things that she was hiding from me, but could I really be mad at her for that? I definitely had some things about myself that I hadn't told her, so did that make us even? Were we both wrong for our secrets and the things that we chose to be untruthful about.

HELL NAW ! her ass just up and eft so as far as I was concerned, the water she was holding was a whole lot worse than and now her ass was playing ghost so I would be Tommy.

I finished Kassidy up and chopped it up with him as usual like we did when we got together. He was a little bit older than me so he always looked out and dropped jewels on me when he could.

"Aite bruh, I'm going to go ahead and get up on out of here," he said, to me as we dapped me up.

"Stay up bro and send Bliss and the kids my love," I said, and Kassidy beamed at just the mention of his family before walking out.

No soon as he walked out Flame walked in, swaggering in late as usual knowing that he had two clients already waiting on him. Everyone being back at the shop as a good feeling. The only person missing was Kiyan because he was at the hospital.

Flame hugged Iggy and I before going to sit at his chair. This man had people waiting, but he was not acting like it. One day these customers were going to whip his ss.

"What's up with you? Who shot your dog?" I asked, Flame noticing his somber mood.

He wiped his hand across his face and sighed. "Females, why must they be so stressful?"

"What have you did now?" Iggy asked, already knowing that Flame had a story to tell.

"I didn't do anything Father time. Pia just in her feelings right now and y'all know that's not a good place to be."

"Boy, you haven't even been out for twenty-four hours yet, and I thought you said that you weren't fucking with Pia," I put him on the spot.

"Man, y'all know that detailing shop on Military highway? Well yesterday the lawyer Jank took be there and low and behold, I see Pia. Long story short, she was pissed that I was even with Stephany and Stephany was doing some weird shit, acting like it was more than what it was between me and her Shit was bogus as hell."

"And why do you think she feels that way?" Iggy asked sarcastically. "You was letting that girl drive you around and to her that meant something totally different than what it meant to you."

"Shit crazy and now Pia is mad put me out her crib and everything."

I laughed. "That is what you get."

"Man, I didn't even do anything for real this time. I could be mad at her ass, when I got there, she was laughing in some niggas face. I let that shit go though because I'm an adult."

Iggy and I both started laughing. This man claimed Pia was in her feeling but I'm sure they may have crossed each other's paths because he was in his too.

"So, what you gone do now?" Iggy asked.

"Shit, I'm cooling."

Just as he said that, the bell chimed signaling someone was walking I to the shop and it was Pia. She whizzed by us so fast that I had to do a double take to see if she had even walked by. Meanwhile, Flame was all in her face and she rolled her eyes in his direction before going to her back room.

"Dayyyuuumm! Yeah, she is mad-mad son," I commented.

"Yeah, and her mad ass will be okay. I might go get her a bracelet or something," he said nonchalantly.

"A bracelet!" Iggy and I said simultaneously.

"Yeah ice her out a little bit. That should help. Female love ice. Isn't that what that bitch Kash Doll keep screaming about, her needing to be iced out."

I ignored what he was saying and made my way to the bathroom in the back. I noticed that Pia's door was half way open and she was whispering. Not one to be a nosey ass nigga, I kept to where I was going until I heard her say Elle's name. I put my ear to her half close door and listened.

"Well, I'm glad that you are doing okay, but you need to come back," I heard her say.

"Elle, I know that damn well you don't want to spend the rest of your life in Ohio."

That shit almost took me out. Elle was in Ohio, but for what? I ease dropped on the rest of the conversation which didn't last that long and it consisted of the two of them going back and forth. Little did Elle know, but she would be seeing me and soon!

FANCY BAPTIST

~~~~~

I looked over the marvelous home with my stager and was surprised that it came this far. I was in the real-estate industry, but I wasn't into flipping until one of my partners presented me with an opportunity. Now here we are three months and two hundred thousand dollars later and I have flipped my first home and people would be piling in for an open house in just a few minutes.

"We did it girl," my partner Shantel gave me a shoulder squeeze.

"Yes!" I said, with a sigh. "Now all we have to do is sell this baby."

If this house sold, Shantel, our other partner Brian and me would be getting a thirteen thousand dollar commission.

I went to the kitchen to get some finger foods before the guests arrived and within fifteen minutes a few families had rolled in. Shantel took the liberty of showing them around while I sat down for a moment. Since, I had found out that I was pregnant, my work load hadn't slowed down, but more now than ever I was starting to feel the effects of my pregnancy. My feet were protruding out of my shoes, my hips were spreading, and my clothing fit just a little tighter than they did before.

⁕ As soon as I sat down, I heard the doorbell ring and got up to answer it. When I opened the door, I was met with a bouquet of white roses, my favorite. Kiyan moved the roses showcasing his handsome face, stepping inside.

"KB, aww thank you," I took the roses and sat them on a nearby table. They were so beautiful and if I wasn't already having a good day ,this just made it ten time more special. Kiyan was never this person in our relationship, in fact this person rarely showed up. It seemed like when we first met things went downhill fast and then he straightened up only to fuck up again.

Now, since we had decided to really give our marriage an honest try, Kiyan was proving to be the man that I always wished he could be. It was scary though because now I was just waiting for the other shoe to drop. I always wondered if he was just playing nice because I was pregnant and then once the baby Came, he would switch up on me. That was something that came across my mind every now and then, but I just prayed that he had really changed this time.

Kiyan placed a delicate peck on my cheek before taking a look at the Foyer of the house.

"This looks like a whole new house. Y'all really did the damn thing," he said, as if he was wowed.

"Yep, I'm glad to know that those late nights and early mornings counted for something. I didn't know you would show your face here though and thank you for the Roses."

"This was big for you. You know I had to support," he grabbed me into his arm and kissed my lips.

"Well, come on. Let me show you the house," I grabbed his hand and led him up the stairs. We first reached a Master bedroom, It was equipped high ceilings, a fire place and brand spanking nee shiny hardwood floors.

"You like it?" I asked.

"Yeah, where would you put our bed?" he asked standing in the middle of the room.

"Our bed? You mean a bed. I think I would leave it just the way it is," the Stager had decorated the home to a T.

"No, I meant our bed, because I bought the house," he reached into his pockets and pulled out a key before giggling it in the air.

"What!" I asked, trying to make sure I heard him correctly the first time.

"This is our home babe. We are now proud homeowners."

I know the people who were in the home probably thought that someone was dying because I screamed, like literally screamed before jumping into Kiyan's arms. He had really surprised me in a huge way.

"Kiyan, you better not be joking."

He put his hand in the air, "I promise it's ours."

I couldn't believe that this was my house. This house that I had basically built from the ground up. Everything in the home was because of me from the paint used to coat the walls to the Subway tiles.

"When did you do this?" I asked, still reeling over the news that he had just given me.

"Today, as soon as it hit the market. I was on it so that means that you and the rest will get your commission, on me."

"Babe, thank you so much, you don't know how much this means to me."

"Prove it," he said, and looked in the direction of the bathroom.

Just then the door opened and a couple with a stroller walked in.

"Saved by the bell," I sighed. Lately Kiyan wanted it morning, noon, and night so I guess what they said about pregnant vagina was true.

I smiled at the couple and felt kind of bad that they were now wasting their time at this open house when the house was already sold.

Kiyan and I walked down the steps, me still smiling because of the generous gift that he had bought for us. Even though he and I both made more than enough money, we had still been renting and since the breakup we still had our own separate apartments. Now, we would officially be moving up like George and Weezy.

I poured him a glass of bubbly and me apple cider and just as we were about to toast, the door was opened, and I knew that I would have to greet our guests being that Shantel was busy with other guest. I met the person as they were coming in and I was surprised, it was Candis. Now I couldn't be sure, but I was surprised that she would be at this open house when I had showed her several house weeks ago on the other side of town. This home was in the Western Branch area of Virginia Beach and before she was looking in Portsmouth.

"Mis Candis, nice seeing you.. again," I said, kind of thrown off guard.

Kiyan walked from the kitchen and when his eyes landed on her, I could tell that he was confused as well. It was written all over his butterscotch colored skin. I found myself lost in his boyishly good looks even in this awkward moment. He was beautiful, in the past some would have called him a pretty boy, but now with his scruffy hair and beard, he resembled more of a businessman with a little southside street him.

"Candis, I'm surprised to see you here," I could tell in Kiyan's tone that it was more of a question than a statement.

"Oh, I'm just here to see this nice house," she said, with a smile that I knew was disingenuous.

"Really? You told me before that you wanted to stay in the Portsmouth area," Kiyan took a sip from his champs.

"Well, this is for my niece, she told me to come and check it out for her." Now she was just getting caught up in her own lies.

Kiyan looked at me, trying to read what I was thinking and I'm sure he knew that it was just what he was thinking.

"Okay, so show yourself around," I said, remembering that I still had to remain professional no matter how crazy I thought this lady was.

She walked away leaving Kiyan and me.

"This lady is borderline obsessed with you," I whispered to him.

"Be nice, hopefully she will be out of here soon."

A few more people started to come in and while I showed them the house, Kiyan kept himself occupied in the kitchen. Before I knew it to hours had gone by and the house had been shown to at least five families and though they seemed interested they would not get this house unless they generously outbid us.

I started to tidy the place up a bit while Kiyan only stared on like he had something to say.

"A penny for your thoughts?" I asked.

"I'm just thinking about Candis."

She lingered around when you were busy like she had something she wanted to say to me. She had this glossed overlook in her eyes that kind bothered me but was familiar to me at the same time."

"She's clearly developed an unhealth relationship with you. It is weird, she thinks that she's your mother or something."

There was a brief moment of silence and Kiyan looked like he was again in deep thought.

"She's not your mother Kiyan," I said, again so that he could stop feeling sorry for this lady that he didn't even know a month ago.

"I'm not his mother!" I heard from behind me and when turned around Cadis was just standing there like she had been listening to our whole conversation.

"You're right, I'm not his mother, I lost my daughter a long time ago," she repeated herself.

My mouth dropped and when I looked at my husband his stare was blank. Was this lady really walking up in here and saying what I thought she was saying?

"Candis what are you saying?" I asked.

She ignored me and looked at Kiyan. "Kiyan I am your grandmother," she sounded so sincere and a loan tear fell down her face.

We were all speechless and Kiyan just stood there never taking his eyes form Candis. He'd yet to say anything and I know if I was going crazy on the inside, he was one hundred times worse.

"Son, I know this is a lot so I will give you some space, but I have this for you."

She pulled a larch manila envelope from her purse and sat it on the kitchen Island before giving him another look of pity before walking out.

Time stood still for both Kiyan and me for a minute and I walked over to him to console him. My husband had just learned the biggest news of his life and before I knew it, he broke down and just cried.

FLAME BAPTIST

I called Pia for the one hundredth time today only to be sent straight to her voicemail. She was taking her little mad act a little too far and yeah, she was upset, but it was going on day three. Goddamn, a nigga had fucked up, but she acted like she caught me knee deep in the bitch or something. I would give her one more day to cool down before I ran up in her spot.

I made my way to my crib, but I decided to stop at a corner store close to the shop. I needed to pick up some backwoods and some snacks. My big grown ass still had a major sweet tooth. It was the end of August, so the block was still rocking with niggas trying to make a quick buck to keep a roof over their heads.

As soon as I got out of my car, I was approached. It was like a public announcement was put out that I was going to be in the hood today. Numerous kids started to surround my car before I could make it halfway out.

"Flizzy Flame," some them shouted all racing to me to give me dap.

Here I was an average ass nigga and had people looking up to me like this, wanting to show me love.

"What's up y'all!" I greeted them. It HAD to be about six little boys invading my space right now, but I loved it.

"Where you been man?" one of the boys named Sean asked. He was about twelve years old. I had to make up something quick because I didn't want them to know that I was locked up for a lil' minute. Despite the way I moved, I would never want these lil' dudes to think that that going to jail shit was cool. They needed to do more with their lives while staying in school.

"I been around man, but where you been? I know everybody better be getting right for school. Y'all only got a few more weeks."

"You know I'm ready," a kid named Eric said. "I'm getting them Jays too. Ima be fresh to death."

"And while you fresh, remember that the grades need to be fresher. Girls like smart boys," I said sounding like somebody's parent.

It was true though. I didn't want them to succumb to all that living in the hood had to offer. All of these lil' dudes were smart and needed to be focused on school and getting out the hood.

I pulled out a few bills and handed it to them searching the crowd for anther familiar face.

"Aye y'all where Memo at?" I asked, and the boys all of a sudden looked around at each other.

"Why y'all looking crazy? Where he at?"

Once again, they all looked at one another before their eyes fell to the ground. Now, I knew that there was something that they weren't telling me.

"Y'all lil' asses better speak up or hand that money back," I stressed, knowing damn well that I would nerve take something back from them that I had given to them from the heart.

I looked to Sean because I knew that he would never lie to me.

"Yo Sean, where Memo at? I know you know so don't lie."

"He around somewhere?" he shrugged, and looked everywhere, but my face.

"So, now you a liar now?" I asked seriously.

"No, I'm not," he bucked up like he had something to prove.

"He been doing him lately. None of us even hang with him."

"Why not?"

"Just tell him Sean. He gone find out anyway," Eric spoke up just as tired as I was of spinning on this merry-go-round.

"Memo been wilding' lately and he been—" his words trailed off.

"He been what?" Now I was getting pissed off because whatever it was it wasn't that damn bad that he couldn't tell me.

"He been copping," he finally spat out and I had to get him to repeat himself to make sure that I heard him right. I just knew that he wasn't telling me that this fourteen-year-old boy was copping work from somebody.

"Copping what?" I asked, calmly not trying to let the boys see that deadly side of me. "Weed?"

"Nah, he been copping dope."

I ran my had across my face and let out a frustrated sigh. This shit couldn't be true because everyone knew what the deal was when it came to serving kids. That is the one thing that was asked of the local dealers. You didn't sell to Kids and the elderly PERIOD!

"Who he copping from?"

"We don't know," they all shrugged, and I knew that they were being truthful because we had had this conversation countless times before. I didn't care about a little weed, but they knew that anything else was a no go.

"Y'all copping too??" I asked.

"Naw, I swear," Eric spoke and the rest of them followed suit shaking their heads from left to right.

"We promise, Flame. We know that shit not cool."

"If y'all hear anything about this shit, y'all make sure I'm the first person y'all call," I made clear. "And whoever put their eyes on Memo first, come find me."

I talked to the boys a little while longer and then said my goodbyes. The shit that I had just heard me steaming'. Whoever thought that it was cool to sever to a fucking kid would definitely feel my wrath. The culprit would get dealt with and Memo ass would too. Now I had to deal with this shit on top of Pia's fucked up ass attitude. I guess this was my official welcome home.

ELLE LONDON

It had been a few days since the Kissing gate situation that happened with Lex and surprisingly, we were able to move on like nothing happened. He knew how I felt so that was the only thing that mattered. As long as he didn't ever try to kiss me again, we would be good. Just thinking about it made me bust out laughing as I drove to his house.

We were going out to dinner and I would be driving. Now, I know y'all are wondering why would be going out after that, but a girl like me never turns down food and he wanted to take me out just so things wouldn't seem so awkward between up. Sherry told me that I may have been sending him mixed signals, but I didn't think so .Lex knew that I wasn't into him so this would be a friendly dinner, nothing more.

I made my way to where he was which was about twenty minutes away from me. Right now, he was staying with his cousin just like I was. Avant's *Separated* flowed through the speakers of Sherry's Acura.

> *I don't want to be with you, put that on everything I own*
> *(mmm, mmm, mmm, mmm, mmm)*

TESHERA C.

> *I can't believe I stayed around that damn long (mmm, mmm, mmm, mmm, mmm)*
> *If I never see you again, I won't be mad at all (mmm, mmm, mmm, mmm, mmm) no no*
> *'Cause I believe that you're my downfall (mmm, mmm, mmm, mmm, mmm)*
> *You did me wrong (you did me wrong)*
> *I thought you were true (yeah)*
> *You ran out of my life*
> *And now I'm so through with you*
> *I wanted you to be there*
> *Right here with me, oh*
> *And when we were together*
> *We never turned our backs on each other (over now)*
> *But now that we're separated (oh yeah)*
> *We can't stand one another (baby, tell me why, why, why, why, why)*
> *And when we were together*
> *We never turned our backs on each other (oh ooh)*
> *Oh, oh oh, oh, but now that we're separated*
> *We can't stand one another (it's really over babe)*
> *Because you did me wrong*
> *You did me wrong*
> *I thought you were true (yeah)*
> *You ran out of my life*
> *I'm so through with you*

I don't know why every time I turned on the radio, the soundtrack to my life was playing. As if I couldn't get Smoke out of my mind before I definitely couldn't now. Avant was saying some real shit in this sound and I'm sure this is how Smoke thought of me.

Reframing my thoughts, I tried to get Smoke out of my mind by focusing on my future. I couldn't keep living the way that I was, so I had to find a job, start to believe in myself and move on. I rounded the corner of Denmark and the gps let me know that I was nearing my destination.

I pulled up to a white little house that stood on the end of the street. I texted Lex to let him know that I was outside, and he told me to come in. I didn't know why he was telling me to come in when I let him know that I was on my way an hour ago. Against my better judgement lifted myself from my car and went in anyway.

I didn't even have to knock before the door was swung open and a girl let me in. I smiled politely and greeted her and she only smirked. I was guessing that she was Lex's cousin.

All she said was, "You can sit here." She pointed to the basic gray and black leather sectional that I had seen in countless homes before. I sat on the couch and clasped my hands together and took in the scenery of the home. There were several pictures aligned on the walls along with various plants and glassed animals. To say that there was just too much going on was an understatement.

The girl came back a few minutes later, "You want something to drink or something?" she asked.

"Um, sure. Water will be fine," I answered back.

A few seconds later she emerged from the kitchen and handed me a glass of something dark, "We ain't have no cold water and I know you too good for facet water. I just made this tea," she handed me the glass and then walked away.

Attitude much!

I hesitantly took a sip of the tea and it was good. Not like that diabetes crap that McDonalds served. I didn't even know how thirsty I was and before I knew it, I had drunk the who glass.

I looked up at the wall clock and I noticed that I had bene sitting out here for ten minutes, I was about to send Lex another text because my stomach was growling, I was just tired of waiting on him, when he finally appeared.

"About time," I said, standing and stretching my limbs.

"Girl, it ain't been that long," he joked.

"Yes, it has, and now I have to pee. Do you mind if I use your bathroom?"

"Yes, it's back there," he pointed to the rear of the home.

I walked through the living room and I reached the dining room. There was more picture that clung to the walls and I found myself staring deeply into them. I even spotted Lex in a few, but my eyes lingered on one picture that he was in. It was a jail picture with about four inmates in orange jumpsuits.

I scanned the picture from person to person and when my eyes finally landed on the last person, my heart stopped. My palms started to perspire, and my knees felt like that were about to give out underneath me. I couldn't take my eyes from the picture even when I tried. My feet felt like they were planted into quicksand making it hard for me to move an inch.

Something was wrong, I didn't know what it was, but them my vision became blurred and when I peered up, Lex was standing in the doorway, just staring at me. I was seeing him in three's, but I recognized his sinister smile right before I hit the ground and everything went black.

I woke up to darkness only the sound of ringing in my head. I rubbed my head with a sigh, wishing the pain away. I don't know it I was clocked upside my head or what, but I couldn't stop the ringing. I got up to reach for a light switch or something because it was literally pitch black. I fumbled in the gloom tripping over my own feet several times before I finally reached a wall. I skimmed over it with my hand trying to find a switch, but there was no such luck. I felt in my pockets for my phone, but that was gone and it finally donned on me that today would probably be my last day on earth. Once I had saw my ex Que in that picture along with Lex, I knew that I had been set up, but what I didn't get was how Lex had even found me.

When I was dating Que, I had seen all of his family and friends, or so I thought. I sank in defeat falling on the cold hard ground and curled up in the fetus position. After all of the running I had did from both Que and Smoke, today would finally be the end to my running. I'm sure that Que had put Lex up to whatever he had in store for me.

Suddenly, I heard a door open and heavy footsteps started to descend stairs. Was I in a basement or something? My thoughts started to run crazy again and I reached for anything to protect myself with. The light was finally cut on and I shielded my eyes from the light that was blinding me. It was so bright that I could barely open my eyes to try to adjust to it. I then felt myself being yanked up to my feet and finally opening my eyes, I was met with the familiar eyes of Lex.

He pushed me back on a nearby couch and I was finally able to take in my surroundings. Like I thought before, I was indeed in a basement that was damn near empty beside the couch that I was sitting on and the floor that was coated with plastic liner.

"I' m, glad that you finally decided to wake up to join the party," he stared at me with Malice in his eyes sensing my fear.

"Lex what are you going to do to me?" I asked, trembling with trepidation.

"Well, I think that you already know that."

"So, this whole thing was a ploy? You never liked my like I liked you?" I asked, trying to appeal to his emotions.

"I did like you bitch and I was almost thrown off course, but you know what they say, Family first," he said, with a shrug of his shoulders. He then placed the barrel of his gun to my forehead.

"Lex don't do this," I pleaded. "Que doesn't care about anyone but himself."

"Oh, trust I know that, but Que looked out for me when we were locked up together and for that I owe him with my life and if that means eliminating you then so be it. I followed you for months, from Virginia to North Carolina and now here and frankly you are tiering me."

"Lex, please don't do this."

"I'M PREGNANT!" I shouted out, hoping to stall him.

"Bitch you think I give a fuck. I'm not no fucking social worker," he shouted.

I closed my eyes for a moment and said a silent prayer, hoping that when this man shot my life out, I would go to heaven after all of the shit that I had done in life.

When I re-opened them, I felt myself being lifted by my throat off

TESHERA C.

of the couch until my feet were dangling from the ground, my dress was even lifting, and suddenly, the sight that I saw made me shrike right before I heard a cracking sound followed by Lex falling to the floor. Smoke had crept up on him and snapped his neck with his bare hand and I didn't know whether to be relived or terrified.

SMOKE BAPTIST

Without any problem, Elle's parents had given me the address to her cousins in Ohio. I hopped on the first that I could find, not even knowing what I would say to Elle when I finally got to her. I was fucked up about her leaving, but at the same time I wanted to snap her fucking neck for leaving.

As soon as I pulled up to her cousin's spot and knocked on the door, she knew who I was. She was full of giggles and smiles letting me know that her cousin was so in love with me and some more. Finally, after twenty minutes of her talking non-stop, she gave me the address to where Elle's friend lived. It was a good thing, girls did that shit, letting their friends know where they were because if not, I probably would've been driving in circles.

I reached the address just as the sun was falling. It looked like a pretty secluded area with modest apartment and single-family homes. I knew that I was in the right place because Sherry had told me to look out for her gold Acura and there I saw it parked at the end of the street.

I knocked firmly on the front door, and though I heard the TV blasting, no one answered the door. If I had to knock on this bitch all night I would. Finally, the door was opened by a chick with an attitude, but she fixed her face once she saw me.

"Is Elle here?" I asked getting straight to the point. I didn't have time to be smiling with this girl all night.

"Um, no you must have the wrong house," she said, sweetly.

"Well, is Lex here?"

I saw the smile disappear from her face and she lied and said no. She must've thought that I was a lil' gump ass nigga or something because she tried shutting the door and I pushed it back open with so much force that she fell to the ground.

"Look, I don't want to hurt you, but I will." That is all that I needed to say before she pointed to an awkward side door. I went to open it and I saw that there were stairs that I had to go down. I didn't even take the liberty of tying the bitch up because knew that she wouldn't do anything, just by how quickly she pointed the basement out to me.

I could hear voices as I crept the basement steps when I heard Elle's voice get elevated. I knew that it was her from her from the mousey tone. She was crouched down on a dirty looking sofa while some man was standing over her. I listened before approached the two. When he said something about being locked up with her ex, I knew that he was about to do some damage.

He lifted her from the couch, with one hand around her throat. But he didn't know that my grimy ass was right behind him. Elle saw me first and I motioned to her with my eyes to keep quiet. Her eyes were blood shot red and she was gasping for air when I snapped this man's neck. He dropped instantly and so did Elle.

She was breathing frantically and rubbing her neck. I could still see his hand indentations on her chocolate skin when she finally looked up at me, like she was looking at a stranger. In this moment I didn't even know what to say knowing that if I hadn't come she would have lost her life. It made me wonder if Her ex was the reason that she was running, but I quickly erased all of that going back to what she had just said to Lex.

"Elle, you pregnant?" I asked.

She didn't say anything, and she instead raised her dress and there indeed was a little bump. I shook my head before I dropped it into my hands. I wondered what Elle's plan was. Was she just going to go on forever without letting me know that she was having a baby that was possibly mine.

"Shameer," she finally spoke barley above a whisper.

I couldn't even stand the sight of her and I was upset with myself in the moment that I didn't let the nigga murk her lying ass.

"Get up, let's go," I said to her before climbing the stairs. I had forgot about ole girl.

I made it easy for her killing her the same way I did Lex. Didn't even feel bad because I'm sure she knew what Lex was about to do to Elle and she was going to let it happen. I couldn't leave any witnesses when I had just murdered someone so for that she had to go too. When Elle finally came outside, she looked like she was freaking out after seeing two dead bodies, but she would just have to get over her shock.

"Drive straight to your cousins house and get your shit together," I demanded. I pulled her plane ticket out of my car and handed it to her.

"If you are not back in VA by tomorrow, I will find you and next time I will spare not leniency on you," she nodded her head and I pulled off praying that this girl wouldn't treat me. We had a lot that we needed to talk about, but for now all I wanted was some shuteye.

PIA KENNEDY

*I*magine my surprise coming home from doing some shopping and seeing Elle sitting on my porch. This girl had a weird way of just disappearing and then popping up again without any notice. She looked like she had been crying and there was something else that was different about her that I couldn't put my finger on.

"Elle, when did you get here?" I asked helping her into the house. It was early in the morning and blazing outside and I didn't know how long she had been sitting on my porch seeing that I had been gone for hours.

I got her a bottled water and then we settled in the living room on the couch.

"My Life is in shambles right now and I don't know what to do."

"Elle, slow down and tell me what happened," I stopped her. She was rambling on and not even taking a breath.

She looked up at me and I could tell that whatever she was going through it, she even was looked like she was scared like someone was going to do something to her.

"Elle, you are okay, no one is going to do anything to you. Do you want me to call Smoke?"

"NO!" she shouted, to the point where it scared the hell out of me.

"Why not?" I asked.

"I think he wants to kill me too," she said, frantically to the point where I thought that she was hallucinating or something.

"Elle, I think that you need some rest. Come on let's go to the spare bedroom," I said, leading her down the hall. She was still rambling up until she laid down in the bed and instantly, she fell asleep. I knew that she was tired because why in the world would she think that Smoke would kill her and then she said too as if he had killed someone else.

Just as I shut the bedroom door, I heard the sound of my alarm chiming, letting me know that someone had entered my home. I walked to the front entrance and automatically turned back around.

"Pia, I gave you some time. You want to talk or not?" Flame asked, following me into the kitchen.

"You want to talk, then talk," I said, giving him the floor because I didn't have anything to say.

"I'm sorry," he offered.

"And?" I asked, when he didn't say anything else.

"I fired the bitch Elle; I'm not fucking with her like that and I never was."

"Who your little Becky?" I sked, with a smirk because that's exactly what she was. Beyoncé warned us about these hoes.

A part of me wanted to just go what he was saying because I had missed him, but another part of me was still mad about his dishonesty.

Did Darnell forgive Mya? Did Melanie forgive Derwin? Yesssss!

"So, can we just make up and be nice to each other," he said ,walking closer to me.

I Put my hand out to stop him and it hit his chest.

"Back up playa'. I forgive you, but I am still mad at you," I said, still trying to play hard knowing that it had been a long time since I felt him inside of me.

In one swift motion, Flame lifted me up onto the kitchen counter and before I knew it he was rubbing my pulsating clit.

"Wa... wa... wait," I managed to get out. "Elle is here."

He scrunched his face up, "When the hell she get back?"

"Today," I said, breathlessly.

Shook his head for a moment and then returned to his task at hand. He lifted my shirt over my head and massaged my nipples with his tongue in a circular motion.

I let out a loud moan and I had to remember that Elle was just down the hall.

"Wait, Fame, maybe we should wait until she leaves," I suggested knowing that was not what I wanted to do, but I also didn't want her to walk out and catch me fucking.

"Pia, I don't think you understand this, but I was locked up for damn near three months and ain't had no ass since. Ain't no better time than the present."

I didn't even protest as he pulled my panties to the side and lowered himself so that they were face to face.

"Pretty ass pussy," he looked up at me for a second before tongue kissing my slippery pearl. He wasn't even a minute into doing what he was doing and I felt myself on the verge of Cuming. Flame flicked his tongue in and out of me while using his fingers so that his tongue could gain access to my pink center.

I braced myself on the island while one foot was propped on Flames shoulder. "Shhhhh shhiitt," I stuttered out at this point not even giving a damn that Elle was in my home. She would just have to bear with this ecstasy that I was in right now.

"Ride my tongue," Flame managed to get out and I did just as he told me to do. I grinded my hips onto his face, my juices making a swoosh sound, sticking to his face. The minute I came, Flame was expecting it and he caught every drop, wiping me clean with his mouth.

I pulled him up to me and this man was smiling like he had just found gold, before he intensely kissed my lips.

"I will kill a nigga behind this good ass pussy," he said, before filling me up with all of him. He sat me on the counter and ease himself in and out of me, each time increasing the intensity of his stroke. This felling that I was experiencing was so good that I could cry as I pumped my hips on to his torso making our bodies collided into one another.

"DAYUMMM BOY!" I screeched, never wanting this moment to end. It was like after all of the fighting and even the distance, our bodies were still so in sync with one another. We moved in unison and created a melody only the two of us knew.

"I'm about to nut, P," I heard him say lowly in my ear.

"Let me catch it," I said, and then jumped down from the counter dropping to my knees. I took Flame into my mouth, delighting in his girth. His dick swam in my throat and I used the tow hand method twisting on it along the way. Flame was palming my head the entire time forcing more and more of his dick into my mouth before he came and released himself down my throat. I swallowed his warm babies until there was no more.

Yanking me from the floor, he looked me into my eyes, "You don't have any other bitch to worry about. It's always gone be me and you," he offered me.

I guess that was his way of making me feel secure, but there would always be a tiny doubt that I held when it came to Flame, just a tiny piece. We showered or called ourselves showering before Flame had me swinging form the shower rod like MeMe.

"Flame," I called out as I lotioned his back after we got out. "Elle said something weird today, she said that she was afraid that Smoke would kill her. And get this she kind of inferred that he may have killed before."

Flame tensed up a bit when I mentioned that before his phone started to ring. He answered it and whoever it was got his attention very quickly.

He looked over to me when he hung up, "I have to roll out really quick."

I stopped him before he could even finish, This was legit our first time that we had had time together since he had come home and now look.

"Really Kindal!"

"I know our trust is fucked up right now but believe me when I say it's really some shit that I have to handle."

"So, let me come," I threw at him knowing that he would dead my ass.

"Pia, stop talking crazy. You know that's not going to happened."

"Kindal, you think that I'm dumb. I know that you have some other things going on other than owning a barbershop. I see the way you move and right now there is nothing stopping me from thinking that it is another woman," I folded my arms, fed up with his lies. I chose not to say anything before, but I knew that he and his brothers were probably down with something shady.

'Pia, this isn't up for discussion. Now I got to go, he said to me like he was my daddy or something.

"Okay, and don't come back," I was serious this time. If he couldn't be honest with me, then I didn't need him in my life.

"Damn man!" he snapped. "Get dressed and bring your crying ass Pia."

I jumped up and slid on leggings and a t-shirt.

"And if you see something that you don't like, it's on you," was the last thing he said before we left to go to go mind his business.

FLAME BAPTIST

Pia was typing away on her phone, feet curled all up on my leather and everything. I figured that she could roll with me this one time to ease her mind from thinking that I was fucking around. I had just got the call that Memo was spotted on the Southside, so I knew that this was the perfect time to confront him about the shit that I had been hearing.

It was about seven pm and the sun was still peeking out just a little so I wanted to make tis quick so that I could get Pia's nosey self in the house. The low sun shining against the against the passenger window made her look like she was glowing. I couldn't help but continue to sneak peeks of her taking in her timeless beauty. The baby hairs were tucked just right, and a lone dimple sat on the left side of her face. She probably didn't remember, but I meant what I said when I compared the feeling of being with her to when I counted my first mill. I felt that way then and I still feel it now.

I reached my destination and I thought about leaving Pia in the car, but I knew that that would cause further friction between us, so I decided to take her in with me. Wont shit gone pop off anyway and if it did I had a burner and a fresh pack of matches.

"Where are we?" she asked when we parked. I forgot she was from the beach and didn't know shit about these parts.

"Don't look sacred now. Yo ass begged to come, now come on," I joked.

She hopped out of the car running to me and clutching my side making me chortle.

We walked down the block until I reached where Memo's mama stayed. I didn't even have to knock because the door was halfway open. I walked in to the TV blasting in the darkly lit living room. Various kids were sprawled out on the floor sleeping and I figured that Memo's mama was babysitting her grandkids or lack thereof. She sat on the couch head hanging low, nodding every couple of seconds. Here she was high as a kite and was responsible for her underaged son and grandkid. I shook my head in Dismay.

Pia looked on like she wanted to say something but chose not to. She wasn't from the hood and neither was I, but I'm sure she had seen her fair share of hood shit. I led her to the stairs and marched up them with her on my heels. The shit was comical to see her sassy independent self all up on a nigga.

I walked from room to room in search of Memo, before I finally found him and the rumors were confirmed. This nigga was nodding, saliva dripping from his lips and some more. He didn't even hear me come into the room, that's how high he was. The shit had me livid to think of how this fourteen-year-old boy's life could be possibly ruined because niggas ain't have no morals and sold drugs to kids.

I kicked the chair that he was sting on and he looked up for a moment and then went right back to nodding. I kicked the chair again, but this time much firmer and if I had to do it again, he was gone feel this size ten up his ass.

"What the fuck man!" he cursed.

"What the fuck is right nigga! Get your ass up."

When he realized that it was me, he straightened up.

"Flame, what are you doing here man?" he asked with a lazy smile, trying to give me dap.

I smacked his hand. "I'm asking the questions. Hell you doing getting high?"

"Ain't nobody getting high Flame," he said barely able to keep his head up and lying through his teeth.

I yanked his ass up from the chair so that we could be face to face. Since, he thought he was a man, he would have to face me like one. I looked back and Pia stood there kind of shook, she had never seen this side of me.

"So, stand right here and tell me to my face that yo' ass ain't high on dope right now?"

He shook his head slowly, but that weak ass smile had disappeared.

"It was only a few times," I promise.

"A few times?" I asked, with my teeth clenched. "You not supposed to be doing that shit at all. You know this shit fuck up people lives? Why would you even to get yourself hooked on this shit," I let him go and eh dropped to the floor, a pile of clothes breaking his fall.

"I'm not hooked Flame, I promise. I just do this shit to deal sometimes."

"Deal with what? What are you going through that is that bad?"

"Everything man, shit just hard for me," he said, trying to gain some sympathy, but I wasn't there with him yet.

"Tighten up Memo. Ima give it to you raw. Its people that done been though worse shit than you so that shit ain't no excuse. I'm not even gone get into the shit I went through as a kid, but I know for a fact it was worse than what you going through. The difference between you and me though, is that you have people that can help you. I know your mama got her own shit going on, Yeezy's and J's, you couldn't tell us what you were going through?" I asked, calming down a bit.

"Man, I just didn't want y'all to be mad at me. I'm fucked up Flame," he finally admitted breaking down.

"Memo, I'm not mad at you man, but I am disappointed. Yo got so much shit going for yourself to throw it all away."

There was a moment of silence where we just stared at one

another. Pia looked like she didn't know what to say, but I know she felt bad for Memo.

"Who you are copping you from Mo?" I asked getting to what I really came here for.

"Some nigga from up town," he tried telling me anything.

"What's his name Mo?" I asked firmly.

"His name, Khiri," he said lowly.

"And where he be?"

"Man, he always come to me, but I think he own a car lot or something."

"Alright nuff' said."

"So, this is what's going to happen. I'm going to come and get you tomorrow and you carrying yo' ass to a rehab that I found for adolescents."

Memo let out a long sigh, but I didn't give a fuck. He was going.

"Don't try no sneaky shit Memo. If you think that you just about to throw your life a way and sit up in this room and get high, you have another thing coming. You will thank me later," I gave him one last look of pity before I grabbed Pia's hand and walked out.

Pia snuggled close to me as we were walking, "You scarred?" I asked knowing that she had just saw a different side of me.

"Not at all. I'm actually proud of you. You don't have to do what you are doing for Memo, but you are doing it anyway. That is pretty cool," she said, and I could hear the sincerity in her voice.

I didn't want to mess up the moment, but I knew that this was my time to be honest to her about my alternate lifestyle.

"P, I have to tell you something," I said taking her face into my hands.

"No, me first, I have to tell you something and I don't want you to be mad at me."

Just like quick she had me thinking about what was so important that she needed to share with me. I looked he right her eyes and braced myself for what she was about to say.

SANDY MUUGS

"So, you are telling me that you are not going to do it," I walked back and forth cradling the phone between my neck in my ear.

"You are a fucking Pussy Spence. After all of the shit that I've done to help you keep your job?" I couldn't believe what my partner was telling me. It seemed like those Baptist Punks had everyone scared or either on their pay roll.

"Well, fuck you too and that better not go any further than this phone conversation because I have shit on your ass too," I hung up right in his ear and tossed my burner phone on the couch. I was officially fucked. All of my plans to get the Baptists had backfired on me and Spence's bitch ass bounced out on me at the last minute.

Just then Charles walked in easing my mind just a little. I swear he could light up my darkest days just by his mere presence.

"What up with you stinky feet?" he greeted me full of jokes as usual.

"Nothing, just sitting here thinking."

"Anything I can help you with?"

I looked at him for a minute wondering if I could trust him to pull off what I needed him to. We had been rocking for a few weeks and he proved to be loyal so far so I wondered if I could take it to the next level with him.

"Naw, I'm good," I ultimately decided not wanting to scare him off.

"You don't trust me do you? Every time I ask you something, you shut me down like I'm a lil' nigga or something."

He had really said that with his chest showing me a different side of him. Usually he handled me gently, but I kind of like this side to him.

"I didn't mean to do all that, but for real if we are going to be together, you are going to have to start trusting me more," he said stroking my back.

"I hear what you are saying, and I do trust you, but..."

"But what, let me help you and be down for you."

He was really laying it on thick and as badly as I could use his help, I didn't want to get him involved. He didn't know, but I was actually being selfless. If he were anyone else, I definitely would have sent him in on the dummy mission. I would just have to handle this situation delicately and by myself.

"How about you worry about what's right in front of your face," I said, with lust all through my voice. I got on his lap and straddled him hoping that it would take his mind off wanting to help me. Fucking me to sleep is where I really needed his help so hopefully, he would be up for the task.

SMOKE BAPTIST

My brother texted me letting me know that Elle was squatting at Pia's house so that was my first destination in sight. I doubted that she would even come back, but she knew that I was serious and doing anything else other than would I told her would result in chaos.

I sat in my car sitting in front of Pia's house trying to calm myself down before I went in and faced her. At this point, I wasn't even thinking about her just up and leaving, but the fact that she was pregnant. I braced myself for what was to come and walked inside of the house. Pia and Flame were still out so we would have this time to ourselves.

I walked into the house and only one light peeked through the leading me to a bedroom at the end of the hall. The door was slightly ajar and I could hear the shower running before it cut off. I could see that the bed had been slept in so I knew that this was the place where Elle had occupied. Walking into towards the bathroom I looked through the cracked door before the water suddenly cut off.

Elle stepped out of the shower holding on to the side rail so that she wouldn't fall. She was still so tiny and even though I was mad, I could help but smile at her little round baby bump. She grabbed the towel that sat on the toilet all the while I couldn't take my eyes off of her as she towel dried her body stopping at her stomach. She rubbed it gently as if the baby could feel it and I could have sworn I saw her crack a smile before wrapping the fluffy pink towel around her body.

I knew then I didn't want to be caught looking like a creep so I backed away from the door. I could hear the sounds of her brushing her teeth before she finally came out. Stunned to see me standing up at the door, she looked around realizing there was nowhere to go. I could see the fear oozing from her which let me know that she guilty about something, but what I didn't know.

"Please don't hurt me. I swear I didn't know. Muggs had things on me too," she rambled on and I tried to make sense of what she was saying.

"Elle, you are going to start from the beginning because I don't now shit you talking about," I looked at her confused by all that she had just spilled.

"So, you don't know what I did?" Now she was the one looking confused.

"Apparently not."

She started to tug at her fingers, and I knew that whatever she had to tell me was the reason that she had left. All along I thought that she was just not ready for a relationship with me, but clearly it was something totally different.

"Well, before I tell you this I want you to know that it had nothing to do with me and you. I actually loved you," she paused and looked at the ground. "And I still do."

"So, before I even met you, my ex Que was into some really shady dealings and somehow he got me involved in it. Muggs was the detective on his case so once Que got sentenced, she tried to come for me telling me that if I didn't give her information on you and your brothers she would try to get me for being an accessory to Que's crimes."

She took a breath after telling me a mouthful and I could hear my

CAUGHT IN A HOT BOY'S FLAME 2: THE BAPTIST BROTHERS

temperature rising. Muggs was like that damn nit that just would not go away until you smashed the bitch.

"And then what?" I replied.

"Then she started to threaten not only me, but my family. I had made up my mind not to help her up until then, I couldn't risk them being hurt so I did what I had to do. On the day of the anniversary of you Foster Parent death, I heard you all talking at your house, so I recorded you, not even knowing what I was going to do with it."

She was now getting really animated when she spoke, her arms were flailing all over the place and her eyes watered with each word she spoked.

"Once, I recorded y'all I knew that I was falling in love with you and I couldn't stand to hurt you or your brothers, so I made a decision to say fuck Muggs and not give her shit. I was willing to face her wrath because you and I had something real. Fast forward to a few days later. She came to my house to let me know that she was going to back off and stop fucking with me, but I made the mistake of trusting her in my home and somehow she got the recording form my phone and ultimately that is why your brother is in jail," she said with her head hung low.

I just looked on, taken aback but everything that she had just threw at me. The whole time, we were wondering how Muggs had any kind of recording and it was because of Elle. Now I understand what Pops was trying to tell us before he died. He knew that there was a snake in the grass and the whole time it was the person who is now carrying my child.

"So, that's why you left?" That is all I could muster up to say.

"Yes, I knew that I couldn't face you after that and I am sorry for all of the discord that I have brought into your life. It was never my intention."

"So, I guess your intention was just to let my brother rot in jail while you moved on with your life! Oh, and let's not forget that's my child you carrying. Did you think that you could just keep that shit away from me Elle," I asked, my temper starting to get the best of me?

She stood here with these tears, but not once did she try to make shit right.

"You have to believe me. I didn't know what to do. I ran because that's what I'm good at. Honestly, I don't even have to keep that baby if that's what you want. I found out that I was pregnant when I got to my parents' house and to be honest it was the only thing keeping me going at the time. I knew that I had lost the best thing that ever happened to me and I didn't have anyone else," the tears flowed down her brown cheeks and even after all of the shit that she had done, I would never really be done with her now that she was having my child.

"Elle I'm trying my hardest to maintain my composure right now, but as smart as you are, you are selfish as fuck. You weren't thinking about anybody but yourself when you were making all of these decisions. You didn't think that any of this was shit that you could've talked to me about? You could've got my brother football numbers."

"You have to understand that I was scared. I thought that you would blame me for everything like you are blaming me now."

"Well, you're not blameless in any of this shit you know? And what was up with ole boy back in Ohio?"

She looked up at me with resentment in her eyes, "Ugh, I don't know. We were just friends, but it turns out that he was sent by my ex. I don't know what he would have done to me, if you wouldn't have got there when you did," she sounded relived.

My head was all over the place. A part of me felt like I couldn't trust her and then another part of me feared that she would just up and run again.

"Can you please say something," she said, softly.

"Fuck you want me to say Elle? That shit is all good? That we can move on a be a happy family?"

"No, I don't need you to say any of that. I just can't stand the silence. Yell at me if you want to."

"Elle, I'm not about to sit here an ease your guilt my nigga. You know you foul and instead of just being real with me, you chose not to. You bogus as hell for that and till the baby gets here I don't think we have anything else to talk about, if its mine."

I stood up, sick of wasting my time entertaining her ass.

"Oh, and here you go," I said, before exiting the room.

I dropped the elephant charm bracelet to the ground never looking back.

KIYAN BAPTIST

I examined the contents of the package Candis had given me and to say that I was shocked had to be an understatement. There lied everything about my mother and my birth. I didn't know if this was supposed to be a moment of closure for me or if I would just be opening another can of worms.

There was my birth certificate and the many attempts that my grandmother and mother tried regaining custody of me. I don't know what happened, bit that never happened and ever since then they had been checking for me before my mother's untimely fatal car accident.

All the information that I had retained was what I had longed for forever, but now that I had it, it really didn't know what to do with it. I learned my mother name which was Katrina Sheard and the entire foster care process was. There were also receipts of countless private investigators that my grandmother found to try and track me down. When Katrina gave me up, she was living with her dad, my grandfather and he was the one who made my mother give me up unknowingly to my grandmother.

A part of me felt like I my brothers would think that I was switching up on them if I really gave these people a chance and I would never want them to feel that ways. Yea, I longed yo know my biological family, but no one would ever replace my brothers or my wife. My thoughts started to go back to the thoughts of my childhood and all of the things that I had been through, not just with the Baptists, but my entire childhood in the system. Though I was abused, that never hardened or deterred me from wanting a family and still longing for my biological family. Unlike Flame, who hated his donors, I really didn't know how to feel about mine.

I made up excuse for whoever they were all to ease my pain of no having them. I reasoned in my mind that maybe giving me up was what they thought was best or maybe they would even get their self together and come bac for me one day. Those thought are what kept me going and up until a few years ago, I still believed it.

"Kiyan, are you going to sit and stare at that stuff all night?" Fancy shook me from my thoughts.

"You may as well get a good night's sleep and revisit it again tomorrow."

I decided to take my wife's advice because nothing would come to me tonight, but more questions.

I climbed in bed and curled up with Faye, rubbing her expanding belly. She and I had come so far from a few months ago and I was glad that she didn't give up on me. After, about an hour, sleep still didn't come to me while Fancy snored away. For some reason, my grandmother was still on my mind and as much as I just wanted all of this to go away I knew that it wouldn't.

I quietly got out of bed and grabbed my phone and headed to another room. I found the contact that I was looking for and finally decided to recall Candis's calls. She had called me a few times and I had only sent her to the voicemail not really sure of what to say to her. Before she answered, I took a deep breath and got ready to hear everything that my grandmother had to say.

FLAME BAPTIST

I had just dropped my boy Memo off at the drug rehab where he would stay for the next thirty days. Shit was high as hell, but that didn't matter to me as long as he came out with his head straight. His mam signed him off with no problem, didn't even know what she was signing, and I knew she was part of the reason that his young ass was even getting high. That's all saw him mama do in and out, so I guess he just succumbed to it.

Next on my list of things to do was go pay a visit to the nigga who had vehemently defied me by selling to kids in the first place. Last night when I was talking to Pia, I thought that she was about to drop a bomb on me, but what she really let me know is that she knew who The nigga Khiri was AKA Ri the dude that owned the detailing shop. Memo had said something about a car lot, and Pia put two and two together that he had to have been talking about her lil' boyfriend Ri.

That shit messed me up though because I was about to come clean to her, but when she told me that Ri was the person who was selling to the kids, that was the only thing on my mind. Now, I had to handle this shit and I hopped that we could do it amicably, but if not I was with all the shits.

I pulled up to the detailing shop which looked more like a block party. School was about to start back up in a few days and instead of these mama's spending time with their kids, they were out here half-dressed and assed out looking for a few dollars. I walked amongst the crowd and they parted like the red sea. Even at someone else's establishment, I was still untouchable.

A few niggas from around the way nodded in my direction showing respect while the bitches' eyes me with lust in their eyes. A few months ago, I definitely would have been choosing, but I was locked down, happily. I walked into the office leaving the to see a few niggas siting around lounging. The goofiest clown I spotted was Ri himself with his feet kicked up. I only chuckled and shook my head.

"I need to speak to you ALONE," I stated. The chatter ceased, and all eyes were now on me.

"Whatever you have to say in front of me you can say in front of my partners big man," he joked slapping his dude's hand.

"You are right and this won't be too long anyway. Word is you like selling drugs to kids. That's how you are rocking?"

"Man, we out here eating. Everybody can't charge one hundred dollars for haircuts like you do shawty."

His mans thought that was too funny because they all roared in laughter. Typical clowns, they always knew me when I couldn't give a damn about them.

I sat down in the chair that was closet to me and clasped my hands together, never taking my eyes of Ri. If this nigga wanted to be an example, he could feel the flame.

"Okay, fair enough. But let me just say this clearly so you and your peons can get it. If this little mishap ever happens again, for every piece a work you are selling, I'ma make you eat it. It's just that simple," I shrugged and sat back in the chair.

"Big man calm down. It's this really what you came here for or is it about your girl? I know you still a little hyped about me getting at her, but it's not that deep, she's all yours... now," he still held that cocky smile but behind it, I could sense how uneasy he was. He was just putting on a show.

Again, his crew busted out laughing hyping his scary ass up. All of

TESHERA C.

this shit was for show and I was about to prove it. The moment the calling hyenas shut up it was my time to laugh.

"Ya'll niggas so funny, make me laugh."

They looked around at one another, all four of them.

"You heard me right, I like to laugh too. Make me laugh," I sat back and waited for the show to start.

"You, make me laugh," I pointed to the loudest one who thought that whatever Ri said was oh so funny. His fat ass.

"Nigga, you tripping," he replied, and then turned to his partner only to laugh again.

I reached for my waist and pulled my gat out and sat it on the table in front of me. I actually hated using guns. That was Iggy's thing, but in this moment it was needed.

"Again, make me laugh," I said, now it was my turn to smile cockily.

Fat ass nigga was just looking senseless now with nothing to say. Just like I expected Ri tried to discreetly reach in his drawer to pull his gun out.

"It ant there," I spoke up.

They all looked at me wondering what I was talking about.

"I'm talking to you Ri, that gun you are reaching for not there."

I had cleaned his entire office out last night, he had better be lucky that I didn't burn the bitch down.

"And I know for a fact these weak ass niggas you run with ain't holding, so again make me laugh," I said with a chortle.

How the hell was you pumping iron in the streets and the niggas that he was surrounding his self with wasn't even ready for war. None of these niggas was strapped like they thought they couldn't get got or something. Comfortable ass niggas.

The one I asked to make me laugh was now sweating bullets like a fat black monkey. Now that shit was funny, like funny almost pee on myself funny.

"Y'all niggas tighten up man," I finally stood.

"Ri, I hope my message was warmly received and yo' fat ass still owe me a joke," I said, looking to the black man. "Y'all guys be safe aite ,never mention my girl again nah font do thaaaatt!" I said, with a hint of sarcasm, tapping my gun against his forehead, all Ri did was what I expected him to do, not a damn thing.

PIA KENNEDY

TWO WEEKS LATER

I looked at the News in amazement learning that Ri's shop had burned down to the ground. It was crazy that just a few weeks before that, it was thriving and now it was dust. I kind of felt bad for him, but then when I thought about I didn't really feel that bad after learning that he was selling drugs to kids. That day that I went with Flame, I had never seen anything like that before. Sure, I had saw strung out adults but to see babies addicted to drugs was something that was so gruesome and sad to me.

The news reporter when on and on about the fire while until her segment was over and they were on to the next story. Flame slept comfortably beside me ignoring the fact that I was hooping and hollering about this damn fire. I shook him gently and he ignored by advances and then it got a little rougher. I could tell that he wasn't really sleeping anyway.

"Babe!" I yelled, and he jumped up with a scowl on his face. He hated to be wakened up even if he was fake sleeping.

"Isn't it so crazy that Ri's shop burnt down to the ground, just two weeks after you payed him that visit," I asked, getting up and fastening my robe around my body.

"I don't know," he said, brushing me off and rolling back over.

I thought about the day that he had come clean to me about his childhood and the house fire that his foster parents had died in. Though he hadn't set the fire, he didn't stop it either rightfully so. The wheels in my head were now turning as I wondered if I had indeed been sleeping with the fireman.

Flame could smell me thinking up a storm and he turned over, sat up and faced me.

"You know I would jeopardize anything that you have or implicate you in anything right?" he asked me seriously.

I went and sat beside him not sue of what to say if he was telling me what I thought he was.

We sat quietly for a moment, but our silence spoke volumes. Flame hadn't come out and told me anything, but his silence told me everything that I needed to know.

"So, what now?" he asked as if he was stuck just like I was.

Silence.

"We keep going. As long as that part of your life doesn't affect me, we are good. Just be safe and remember that you can't be the hood vigilante forever," I rested my head on his shoulder and for a moment we just sat, one delicate kiss he placed on my forehead, letting me know that he had heard me.

SMOKE BAPTIST

I finished up my third client of the day and sent him on his way. To keep my mind off of things, I buried myself in work as usual so Smokin' Kutz is where I had had been living for the past few weeks. Occasionally Elle would cross my mind and I would busy myself into doing something so that it could distract me from her. I had decided to keep her little indiscretions to myself because I knew if Flame found out that she had something to do with him getting locked up, I wouldn't hear the end of it.

"So, KB, what's going on with your peoples?" I heard Iggy ask Kiyan. It had been a few weeks since he had had the bomb dropped on him that his grandmother was basically stalking him.

"We talked in depth and she basically told me everything that I need to know. Of course, we are going to take a blood test, but until then we've just been taking things slow."

"That's good to hear man," I chimed in. I was genuinely happy for my brother because a family was all he ever really wanted.

"What's going on with you Iggy?" I turned to him. "And how is Beauty?"

He looked up and smiled. Sprung ass nigga.

"Everything straight on our end. She is getting better and basically want to be up under me all the time, but I love it to be honest."

"Whatttt! Ain't never gone fall I love Iggy really out here with one woman. I never thought that I would see the day brother," Kiyan slapped the back of Iggy's head.

"Hey, we all have to grow up one day and we had the talk," he put emphasis on the talk and Kiyan and I knew exactly what he was talking about.

"And?" I questioned wanting to know how she reacted to learning about his alternate lifestyle.

"And, I'm out the game ghost," he replied mocking his favorite shoe power.

"Whaaaatttt!" I replied stunned.

"Yeah, man. It was either her so it, so I you know what I chose. But between us y'all know that shit gone always be in my blood so if I need to step back in, she does not have to know that," he winked.

I couldn't believe my ears, Ignitus Baptist was really in love for him to make that decision, but I couldn't do anything but salute him for that shit though. It's hard to get in the game, but it's even harder to get out.

"And you? Since you full of questions, you still not talking to run away love," Iggy joked talking about Elle.

"Nah, I'm not even on that," I replied simply.

"What did she do that was so bad?" Kiyan asked. "I know she disappeared for a little minute, but she's back now."

He didn't even know that half and I wasn't about to tell him. The guys didn't even know that she was pregnant, and it was going to stay that way.

"You might as well talk to her man," Iggy offered and it's crazy because his ass was usually the stubborn one.

"Man, I don't have to do shit, Father Time."

"Yes, you do because she's walking this way," Kiyan and Iggy both nodded outside and I saw that Elle was walking up to the shop.

"Baby girl done put on a little weight too," Kiyan and Iggy both had their heads cocked to the side watching her walk up in the colorful sundress that she was wearing. She looked good though.

The bell chimed signaling that she had entered, and I could tell that she was nervous. She waved a shy hello to Iggy and Kiyan before turning to me.

"Can we talk, please?" she asked timidly.

I nodded towards the door following her out.

We got out there she only looked around like she didn't know what to say.

"What's on your mind Elle?" I asked getting a little frustrated.

"Shameer I don't want to be your enemy," she started out.

"You are not my enemy Elle; I just don't trust you."

"I know and I get that, but I don't want us to act like strangers either. Regardless of what you and I have to do, we will have to raise this child together. I guess what I'm trying to say is I just don't want you to resent the baby because of the mistakes that I've made."

She looked up at me towering over her, squinting her eyes from the sun. Three freckles sat on her pointy nose and I could feel the sincerity radiating from her. Yeah, she had fucked up big time and things would probably never be the same between us but, I couldn't stay mad at her forever.

"We're straight Elle, there is no love lost. I not ready to be smiling all in your face yet, but you know I'ma be here for you and the little one and whenever you call I'ma come running."

She smiled a little making me smile to myself.

"And just in case you didn't know, that shit that happened in Ohio."

"Never happened," she finished my sentence.

We stood silently for a while.

"Well, I'm going to get on back in here, I have a customer waiting."

"Okay, I guess I will see you around and thank you for talking to me."

We hugged like this was going to be our last time seeing one another, but I knew that it was deeper than that. I was going to have to be friends with the girl that I was in love with.

I got back to work an before I knew it three hours a flew past right when I was on my last head. The bell chimed again letting me now that someone was entering, like it had been ringing all day. I definitely would have to go back to only cutting four heads a day or two days a week like Flame because this shit was getting outrageous.

I looked p and I was met with the eyes of a familiar stranger. It was the dude that I had saw with Sandy a few weeks back. I immediately stepped to him, Iggy and KB following my lead ready for whatever.

"I come in peace," he held his hands up as if he was surrendering,

"Fuck is this dude?" Kiyan asked, unusually gangster.

"The weakest nigga in America. Guess who this fool is fucking?" I asked with a laugh. "Sandy."

Kiyan and Iggy both fell out laughing. The shit was comical. Sandy looked like a light skinned rat in the face and any nigga who was fucking her was just doing bad.

I was surprised when he Cracked a smile too. He must've knew that he was a gump ass nigga.

"Speak your peace, before piece be steal," Iggy said, going for his girlfriend on his waste.

"Damn, them Baptist boys tough, but I like that. I guess that the reason Sandy hate y'all fucking guts. I'm on y'all team though."

"Again nigga, who are you?" Kiyan asked.

"The nigga that's gone help y'all get rid of that mangy bitch for good, but I have to let y'all know. That Muggs want y'all so bad that she put some shit in your trunk," he pointed to me.

"I don't know what it was, but I bet you it ain't nothing nice. I was following her last night and she pulled up to this shop, popped the trunk and put a bag in this bitch. I knew that it was yours because I remembered your car from when I first seen you at the restaurant."

"And why the fuck should we believe you?" Iggy inquired.

"Man, you don't have to, but I'm the type of man who looks out for the people who look out for me. Sandy spoke about y'all so much that I did my own street research and found out that Flame was y'all's brother. He was locked up with my lil' brother and looked out for him so I thought that I would repay my gratitude. Yeah, I was fucking with Muggs, but it was only to get some shit on her for my brother. She was fucking with him when he was in high school, but she was grown. The folks found out, that my brother was underaged and then the bitch screamed rape, now my brother doing time for some shit that he didn't even do."

This shit had to be a joke. I listen to what ole boy was saying and it was the same shit that Sandy had tried to do to me. The shit was bazar, whole time I thought he was knocking her down because he was with her, but he was only playing her ass.

I'm done with her ass, I got what I needed from her to get my brother out, so I thought that I would just warn y'all. The stupid bitch keep diaries and shit of everything that she does. She crazy as fuck for real.

"Man, this some bullshit," Iggy said out loud. I was glad that it was the end of the day so the shop was packed at all.

"Aye, look man all I have is my word and Scar banks isn't no weak ass nigga so trust my word is bond, but I just came to tell you to lay low blood and take that shit out of your car," he looked at me.

"Damnmit!" I snapped realizing that flame and I had switched cars, just some random shit that we always did since we were little.

"Flame got my car," I said, to my brothers.

Iggy instantly started to try and call his phone, but he didn't answer.

"Man, hopefully y'all can get in touch with him because if he driving, I know for a fact Sandy done had somebody watching the car and there will be a routine stop wherever he is. I heard her talking about the shit on the phone earlier. It should be happening—" he looked down at his watch.

"In about ten minutes."

Iggy got on the phone and tried to call Flame again and again he didn't answer.

"Damn, man this the only person I know who always his phone in his hand have but never answers the bitch," Iggy snapped.

I tried calling Pia too and what do you fucking know, there was no answer.

Shit at this point all I could do was ride out and continue to pray that Muggs wouldn't win again.

FLAME BAPTIST

The red and blue lights flashed behind me and I just knew that they were about to zoom past me or some shit because they had no reason to be stopping me. I looked over at Pia and she looked like she wasn't even fazed. We had just come from the movies and she looked like she was half sleep after eating all them damn nachos.

I looked in my rearview mirror to see that this one police car was still trailing me and it was only me and him on the road.

Should I take this nigga on a chase? Naw P in the car

I reasoned with myself finally stopping on the side of the road. The officer walked towards me slowly brushing his baton against the car. Smoke was gone be pissed if this nigga scratched his fresh paint job on the Phantom.

I rolled down my window, "How can I help you officer?"

"Well, you have a broken taillight," he said cockily. "License and Registration please."

I dug in the glove department and gave him what he asked for. He walked back to his car before coming back over to me. By now Pia was up asking me ninety-nine questions getting on my nerves.

"Sir, I'm going to have to search your vehicle," he said, when he finally reached me.

"Man, for a broken taillight. This shit bogus as hell!" I snapped.

"Kindal, just let him check the car," Pia said in the background.

"I've asked you nicely. The next time I won't be so nice, now step out of the car sir."

I bit my tongue from shooting this pig with his own gun and ending up bac in jail. I stepped on the side of the road and so did Pia.

"Just calm down, everything will be okay," Pia tried to assure me.

"Pia, you not about this life. Stay in your lane pooh," I said, finally sick of hearing her tell me to calm down.

The officer walked to the front of my car to the back before asking me to open the trunk. I did as he asked.

I just looked on as he rummaged through the trunk. When he finally looked up, he didn't look happy at all. He slammed the trunk shut before walking over to me.

"Make sure you get that taillight fixed," was all he said before he got back into his car and drove off.

"Fuck was that about?" I said to myself before driving off myself.

My phone rung and it was Iggy and I hadn't even notices that he had called me about sixty tines in the last hour. I had put my phone on silent at Pia's request while we were at the movies.

"Yo," I answered.

"Man, are you good. We just got some info and as told that you was about to get stopped," I hear Smoke say.

"I just got stopped and how the hell you know that?"

"Man, we just got word that Sandy put some drugs in the car and you was supposed to be getting pulled over."

Now I was confused. "I just got pulled over but wasn't shit in the car. The pigs searched it and all, but who you hear this from again?"

"We will talk about that when we are face to face, I just wanted to make sure you were straight. An angle must've been looking over you because, Sandy put something int that truck last night."

I hung up with Smoke just as confused as I was when I answered for him. How in the hell did Muggs put something in his trunk without me knowing? I had had his car for two days and I had definitely been in the truck a few times.

"What was that all about?" Pia asked all up in that like it was her business.

"I don't even know for real. Some weird shit"

"Like what?"

I shrugged because I was just as clueless as she was.

"You remember that Lane that you told me to stay in earlier?" she asked and looked at she like she was crazy. She just wanted to start an argument over some dumb shit.

"Well, say thank you. "

"What are you talking about now P?" I ran my hands over my face.

"Say thank you, thanks to me staying in my lane pooh. That cop back there didn't find the drugs that Muggs person planted in your car last night. Last night at the shop, I saw this wired unmarked vehicle keep circling the shop. I waited it out and I saw her get out and she used something to open the trunk and then placed a bag inside.

"I waited until she left, grabbed the keys, and looked inside and guess what it was? Kilos and kilos of cocaine. I'm sure it could've got you or Smoke at least fifteen to twenty. I took the bag out, played her game and followed her and I put it right back in her car."

I sat there stunned at what Pia was telling me. This girl had really looked out and could've got herself in trouble all to help me. Shit was dope as hell.

"So, when I was getting on your nerves back there, I knew what I was doing. I Knew that they weren't going to find anything. Now what!" She jumped in my face playfully.

I was so surprised and grateful at the risk that she had taken for me, all I could do was give her props.

"Thank you P. I don't even know what to say, but thank you," I sat there still wowed and thankful for how everything had one down. If they would have found that cocaine on me, I would've surely did fed time so for that, I owed Pia any and everything that I had to give. My Shorty was a real rider.

"You know I got you, and thanks for teaching me the game Ghost," she joked.

"Aite now, don't go around thinking you Griselda Blanco, or something."

"Who?" she asked giving me the blonde look. I couldn't have taught her that much of the game if she didn't know who she was, but that was cool with me. I would never put her in this kind of situation again where she felt like she had to risk her freedom for me. I had a good girl now and that is the way that it would stay.

SMOKE BAPTIST

THREE MONTHS LATER

Green and Yellow balloons floated through the air as Kiyan, Iggy, and I scoffed down Gerber baby food all in an attempt to win the game. Somehow, I had lucked up and got some nasty ass peas and I didn't get how babies ate that shit; it tastes like some shit you would feed to an animal.

"Done," Kiyan raised his empty jar signaling that he had won the game.

"How the hell did I get Peas and this nigga got bananas?" I asked ,being that sore loser that I always had been since we were kids.

"Don't get mad, because my husband is winning all the games," a very pregnant Fancy said form her bedazzled chair.

The day of their baby shower had finally come and though she and KB were waiting until the birth to learn the sex of their baby, they decided to go with a gender-neutral baby shower theme, which was Precious Cargo.

"Y'all are taking these games way to seriously," Pia said, with a laugh.

"Don't worry because this is exactly how I'ma be at our baby shower when I get you knocked up soon," Flame said licking the side of her face. He was crazy as hell and so was she, so they fit perfectly. Flame has told us all about what she had did so even if they were on bad terms, she was gone be my sis for life.

"Lies," Pia said and gave him a look that made him bust out laughing.

"Can we eat already?" I heard Elle whine. Big mama was four months and her once tiny frame was getting bigger and bigger every day.

"Y'all better feed my two pregnant friends!" Beau yelled from Iggy's lap. She was doing better, and she was healthier these days. She had her good and her bad days, but for the most part she was kicking Cancers ass and her and Iggy balanced each other out, she was the cam to his storm.

"I know right, enough games for now, let's eat y'all," Fancy said, getting up from her chair. Kiyan made sure he rushed over to help her.

All of Fancy's family was in attendance and if we didn't have any family, she sure had a lot. There had to be at least thirty people from her side and Kiyan had even invited his peoples. He had been getting to know his grandmother and the rest of the folks on his mothers' side. He was worried about how we would feel but we were all for the shit. If he as good then we were too, but if he wasn't, shit would go a ruckus.

"What do you want big mama, I will make your plate?" I said to Elle.

"Umm, everything," she smiled.

I should have known, her greedy ass wanted everything on the menu. We still weren't together, but we were working on it. The more that I was around her and seeing her pregnant with my kid, it made me want to become more with her, but for now we were just going with the flow.

I walked to where the food was being served just in time to see Scar walking in. Ever since everything went down with Muggs a friendship between us had been forged.

"What's up bruh?" I dapped him up.

"You know me laying low, but this here is my brother Jacob," he introduced me to the boy that was standing shyly behind him. After, he had spent all of the time in jail, Scar had finally got him out with them diaries the Muggs kept. She detailed how the two of them had had a consensual relationship and how she had lied and said he raped her. She was just a nasty low-down crazy hoe.

I dapped the young man up and I could tell that he had been through some things behind that g-wall.

"Flame is over there," I pointed to wear he was, and it seemed like he got a little bit happier. Flame had looked out for him when they were locked up together never knowing that he had an older brother.

"I'm glad he out man, and you know I can't thank you enough for how you came through."

"Ain't no thing, but I'ma go ahead and feast on these Lumpia and pancit, y'all must've knew a nigga was hungry giving me this invite," he joked, placing his gift on the git table and heading for the food.

"We gone find you a girl so she can cook for you one day bruh."

He waved me off making his way to Fancy and Kiyan while Jacob kicked it with Flame.

Things weren't perfect in each of our lives, but I could say that they were happening the way they were supposed to. With Iggy putting his gun down, that made me slow down a bit too, but I knew I was not ready to completely stop dancing. Kiyan claimed he was going into retirement, so that he could focus on becoming a surgeon, but who ever knew with him, he and Fancy were both trained to go so hopefully he kept his promise. And my wild boy Flame, the *fire man* as the streets called him, well.. Flame was always going to be Flame.

Oh, and for Left eye Sandy, she was now where she thought that my brothers and me would end up. A little birdy had made a call to her boss and she had got knocked for the Cocaine that Pia put in her truck. Her ass was awaiting trial now, but for all of the crooked shit that she had done, she was facing thirty years in prison, eighteen of which were mandatory. All of the cases that she had ever worked on were currently under review thanks to her pal, Spence turning on her to save his ass. He let it be known that Muggs had set up over twelve people by planting drugs o them and things of that nature. That bitch was finally gone, and she had the Baptist brother to thank for that. *Clink, clink bitch.*

The End.

NOTE FROM THE BAPTIST BROTHERS

Thank y'all for taking this ride with us, our story is over for now, but you may hear from us in the future. Until then, keep it hot.
 ~ The Baptists

ABOUT THE AUTHOR

Teshera Cooper is a 27-year-old new author who hails from Norfolk, Virginia. She has a bachelor's degree in psychology from Old Dominion University. While she has a passion for mental health and advocates for black excellence that has never stopped her from turning the vivid imagery that consumes her thoughts into short stories. She has been writing short stories since about 14 years old and drew inspiration from her upbringing and from her experiences from growing up in the "hood". Each of the characters that she creates embodies someone that she has encountered; from the dope boys on the street corner to the hot in the pants girl who deep down inside just wants to be loved.

Teshera is devoted to giving her readers a fast paced and gritty thrill ride with a twist of hood love. Writers who have inspired her include, Terri woods, Sista Soulja, Carl Webber, Wahida Clark, Vickie Stranger, K'wan, Ashley & Jaquavis and countless others. The way that they can bring life into their characters with just the stroke of a pen is pure genius and that is what she aspires to do through her writing.

facebook.com/TeelaMarieCooper

instagram.com/Teela_marie18

Royalty Publishing House is now accepting manuscripts from aspiring or experienced urban romance authors!

WHAT MAY PLACE YOU ABOVE THE REST:

Heroes who are the ultimate book bae: strong-willed, maybe a little rough around the edges but willing to risk it all for the woman he loves.

Heroines who are the ultimate match: the girl next door type, not perfect - has her faults but is still a decent person. One who is willing to risk it all for the man she loves.

The rest is up to you! Just be creative, think out of the box, keep it sexy and intriguing!

If you'd like to join the Royal family, send us the first 15K words (60 pages) of your completed manuscript to submissions@royaltypublishinghouse.com

LIKE OUR PAGE!

Be sure to LIKE our Royalty Publishing House page on Facebook!

CPSIA information can be obtained
at www.ICGtesting.com
Printed in the USA
LVHW041656161019
634411LV00006B/778/P